W9-AUW-054

A PERFECT CRIME

A PERFECT CRIME

A YI

Translated by
Anna Holmwood

ONEWORLD

A Oneworld Book

First published in English in North America, Great Britain & Australia by Oneworld Publications, 2015

Originally published in Chinese as 猫和老鼠
by Zhejiang Literary and Arts Press in 2012

A CIP record for this title is available from the British Library

ISBN 978-1-78074-705-7
ISBN 978-1-78074-706-4 (eBook)

Printed and bound by CPI Group (UK) Ltd, Croydon, CR0 4YY

Oneworld Publications
10 Bloomsbury Street
London WC1B 3SR
England

This book has been selected to receive financial assistance from English PEN's PEN Translates! programme. English PEN exists to promote literature and our understanding of it, to uphold writers' freedoms around the world, to campaign against the persecution and imprisonment of writers for stating their views, and to promote the friendly cooperation of writers and the free exchange of ideas. www.englishpen.org

Contents

A Beginning 1

Prelude 13

Build-up 23

Action 37

Execution 47

On the Run I 57

On the Run II 67

On the Run III 79

The Ending 95

The Interrogation 115

The Game 131

In Prison 147

On Trial 159

The Appeal 173

The Verdict 183

Last Words 197

A Beginning

I went to buy glasses today. I reached for a pair of sunglasses first, but the more you try to disguise yourself, the more you stick out, so I chose a pair of normal ones instead. Much better for diverting people's attention. They'd think I was short-sighted, and short-sighted people seem trustworthy.

I also bought some duct tape, which I wrapped around my hand. It was sticky stuff. It took ages for me to tear it off and get my hand clean again.

The day's plans didn't originally include buying clothes, but somehow I found myself entering a shop, having taken pity on the owner. She was in her thirties, short, with a face grey like dried orange peel. She'd just been humiliated by a handsome customer. Everyone likes beautiful things, why shouldn't she want her own boutique? Well, that's what I thought, anyway. But I regretted it as soon as she looked up. Her eyes were submissive, unbearably so, and they trailed after me wherever I went. Just as I was about to leave she addressed me in a funny voice: 'Uncle, I do a good price. Elsewhere it might cost over a thousand. I sell it for a few hundred. Exactly the same stuff. I've got everything you could want.' She pulled out a T-shirt and continued. 'Try this on. If you don't, how'll you know what it looks like? Try it first, we can talk money afterwards.'

There was an edge to her voice. I headed for the mirror and held it up, but I couldn't see any noticeable difference to how I normally looked.

'It really suits you,' she said as I tossed it aside. 'What are you after, then?'

'You don't have what I'm after.'

I made for the door.

'Try me.'

'I can't explain.'

I walked out and she followed like a disappointed dog. Just at that moment, a suit walked past decked out in the latest fashions from the West, a pair of shiny leather shoes and a briefcase under his arm.

'Do you have something like that?' I said.

'Yes, yes,' she breathed.

'Including the shoes and the briefcase?'

'The whole outfit.'

I figured if I looked professional I'd be trusted. I wouldn't get caught.

She went in and riffled around in a cardboard box, watching me all the while, scared that I might leave again. It was all there. She wasn't lying. Only the brief-case was brown. I carried the items into the changing room, tried them on and emerged to check how I looked in the mirror. I spotted some gel on the table.

'Can I borrow a bit?'

'Of course. Go ahead.'

I squeezed a blob into my hand and spread it through my hair so that it shone.

'How old do I look now?'

'Twenty.'

'Tell me the truth.'

'Twenty-six, twenty-seven.'

She couldn't decide if I was satisfied with her answer and looked on anxiously as I headed back to the changing room. The truth was I was still in school. I'd be lucky to be taken for twenty-six.

I came out again and dumped the clothes to one side. I stared at her for about five seconds and then asked, 'How much?'

She jumped up as if I'd just thrown her a life jacket and started tapping on her calculator.

'I'll give you the best discount. Usually it'd be six hundred for the lot, but for you I'll do five eighty.'

'Too much.'

'The best I can do is knock off another twenty, otherwise I won't make any profit.'

'Still too much. I can't afford that.'

'Then you name a price.'

I remembered Ma's instructions: always cut the price in half. But I was even tougher.

'Two hundred.'

'Too little.'

'Two hundred.'

'Uncle, be reasonable. They're yours for four hundred.'

'I've only got two hundred.'

'If I sold all of that for two hundred I wouldn't have a business left. If you only want to buy one item, we can talk.'

I started to leave. Behind me, nothing but silence. It was a strange feeling, like a nasty break-up after which no one is happy. The further I walked the more I believed her, but by then I was too embarrassed to look back. Just as I was about to turn the corner, just as I was certain I'd lost my chance, I heard her call: 'Wait, wait! OK, for you two hundred.'

I saw her waving at me. I waved back at her, smiled sardonically and then walked away.

I got what I wanted. I only had ten *yuan* on me anyway.

At 6.30 that evening, I returned to the military academy compound where I was living with my aunt and uncle. Mr He, our idiot neighbour, was just coming back. Thanks to the state's military benefits, he lived a miserable life. The whole base was an empty tomb. Me and old Mr He were seemingly the only ones living there and yet the gate was guarded 24/7. The academy sent the latest recruits here as part of their military training and they executed their duties well, keeping their backs and limbs ironed stiff. I had been worried that the guards or Mr He might catch me, but they were all robotic fools anyway.

I followed old Mr He upstairs, waited until he shut his door and eased my aunt's open. The shady spirits inside pounced, though I knew the apartment was filled only with nothingness.

I sat staring into space, not sure what to do next to execute my plan. I imagined how in three or five or fifty days I might be in prison. Apparently prisoners are taught a vocation. They spend their time inside working so that when they get out they've got a trade – as cobblers or carpenters, tailors or carvers. All I'd ever learned to do was to masturbate. I went to my room and pulled across the curtains. It was over pretty quickly.

I drifted off, but before long I was awake and couldn't get back to sleep again. I had to find something to do. Deciding to take my chances, I turned on the light, pushed aside an empty cardboard box, moved some flowerpots, magazines and a vase with fake flowers and finally pulled away the tablecloth to reveal my aunt's safe. I stuck the key in and tried to unlock it. After a while I switched off the light and kept trying: darkness sharpens my focus.

Auntie would go mad when she found out the safe had been emptied, of course, but I was going to need money if I was to have any hope of carrying it off. Maybe she'd cry. Mind you, my aunt deserved it. Me and my family didn't owe her or my uncle a cent. The day it had been decided that I was to come to the city to live with them marked one of the most important business deals to have ever been struck in the history of our family. When they were young, Pa did better at school than my uncle, but only one of them could attend university and Pa let his brother go. While he ended up down a mine, getting lung cancer and dying. Someone had to shoulder the guilt, but my aunt was only ever a bus conductor. It's not like she could really take care of me. She always thought of herself as better than us just because she was born in the capital of our province. Ma sent me to live with her with bags full of presents from our home town, but Auntie gave them back, all proud, saying, 'Keep them, keep them. Things are difficult for you lot.' I wanted to shout at her, 'My ma's got more money than you!' After I moved in, I used to spend my days curled up on the balcony. The whole thing was so humiliating, I wished I was dead.

She would turn off the gas when I showered. Sometimes she would promenade up and down in her high heels while I was watching television. She didn't say I couldn't sit on the sofa exactly, but as soon as I got up she would be there, wiping it down. She was like a farmer looking for cow pats to fertilise her fields, and that's exactly what I was to her: a pile of shit.

Her attention had been diverted away from me recently, though. She and my uncle were building a new house and Auntie had to oversee it. Uncle, meanwhile, had been posted to another base, so I was often left on my own, which I'd thought was going to be great. It would be a relief not to have my aunt breathing down my neck. But I quickly realised it doesn't matter where or how you live, the house always wins over you in the end.

I was still jiggling the key. It was stuck and time was slipping away. Suddenly, I heard footsteps outside. They stopped at the door. Then the jangle of keys. Something was being inserted into the lock. The outer metal door clanged. I continued jigging until I realised with a pulse of frustration, pulling at it wildly, that I couldn't get it out. It broke. Auntie was now opening the inner door and I just managed to flip the cloth back over the safe in time, pulling the corner straight. She closed the doors as I put the old magazines and vase back on top. They weren't in the right position, so I shuffled them around before lifting the flowerpot up off the floor. My hands were shaking so violently I nearly dropped it. The curtain was pulled across the doorway, thank God.

A second later, Auntie switched the light on and made for my room. I was lying on the floor, breathing heavily, counting out loud: 'Forty-four, forty-five.' She scooped the curtain up in her hand and poked her head through, not seeing my foot pushing the cardboard box back into place.

'Why have you got the light off?'

She pulled the curtain back, letting the yellow glow flood in.

'I'm doing my push-ups.'

'Wasting your time instead of studying, in other words.'

She forced me to my feet and appeared to be looking for something. Then she casually pushed aside the cardboard box and grabbed the vase. She was probably about to move the flowerpot and magazines, pull off the cloth and check inside the safe. I needed to say something urgently, anything.

But at that moment she turned and said, 'What's the matter? Didn't I tell you to go and study?'

At once my face turned red, but I didn't move.

'Go.'

The order had been issued and I left, wet with sweat. I sat on the edge of the sofa like a prisoner with his head laid out on the guillotine, waiting for her to storm back out and let me have it.

I imagined choking her to death. I wasn't yet sure who I was going to kill, but if anyone, why not her? It would be too easy, though, too expected. I hated her. But she wasn't worth the energy.

When she emerged she was merely stuffing some old clothes into a bag.

'I'm going to visit your uncle and mother tomorrow. Do you need me to bring back some money?' she asked.

'No,' I said.

I collapsed and she left. For a long time afterwards it felt as if she was still there. I went to my room, but it didn't look as if the cloth had been touched.

Prelude

The next morning I checked again on the key broken off in the lock. It looked like a little dick caught in the jaws of a vagina. It struck me that I needed a pair of pliers. I'd buy some on the way back from school.

Today we were having our graduation pictures taken. The light was soft and dappled, which made the campus look cleaner than usual, cheerful even. The pictures were being done under a row of trees. Everyone was gathered together, chatting. I stood by myself. First we were to have our individual shots, then the group photo. I watched my classmate Kong Jie. She was wearing one of her stage outfits, made from white silk, a pink skirt and a blue necktie. She kept running her hands through her sweaty hair. The sun was beating down on us, making her look even whiter, as if she was being photographed in a winter wonderland.

When Kong Jie wasn't in school, her mother followed her everywhere like a pathetic mutt. At least, that's what she told me. After her father died, she became her mother's sole property, locked up indoors, made to repeat scales on the piano like on a production line. Her mother installed herself in the front row of Kong Jie's every performance, examining the audience's reaction at the end before leading her daughter away. Until one time when the entire audience gave Kong Jie a standing ovation and her mother finally pulled her into her arms and wept with happiness.

The only secret Kong Jie ever kept from her mother was the purchase of a little puppy. Or at least it was while she tried to find a way to broach the subject with her. But by the next morning she realised she was never going to be allowed to keep it. Every day she gave it to a different friend to look after, until she came to me. My aunt was away so much she'd barely notice. It was perfect. That is, until I ended up killing it. I got so mad I kicked it, and it died in Kong Jie's arms. She dug it a grave using a spoon, the tears dribbling down her cheeks. I told her someone else did it.

Just then she caught me looking at her and came over, thinking I wanted to speak to her. There was a sweet empathy in her eyes, like a mute gazing on another mute, a deaf person gazing on another deaf person. We'd both lost our fathers. Maybe that was it.

'You look unhappy,' she said.

'It's my aunt.'

I imagined her laid out in the snow, legs open, me hovering over her. My heart thumped. I couldn't bear to look straight into her charcoal eyes, but I tried to stay casual.

'I can't take it any more,' I said, then I walked off.

They'd tacked up some white cloth where the photos were being taken and put a chair in front of it. Someone would sit down and everyone saluted them with their eyes. Then it was my turn. I was already feeling pretty awkward when the photographer looked up over the camera and said, 'You need to brush your hair. It's a mess.'

Laughter erupted around me. My lip quivered, my cheeks flushed, but I straightened up and pointed my chin fuzz right at the lens, clenched my cheeks and stared it down, cold and mean. I wanted this to look like a mugshot. I wasn't trying to look good, this was going to be the image everyone would remember me by. The picture that would be plastered all over the papers. For my aunt and my mother.

When they were done I walked away. I was never going to see this place again.

I had a hundred *yuan* left after buying the pliers. Might as well buy the rope and knife while I was at it. You had to get a certificate to buy a combat weapon, so at first I thought of purchasing a fruit knife, but the shopkeeper gave me a conspiratorial smile and I realised I needn't be so careful. He led me into the back room and took out a box of army switchblades. I chose the cheapest one. I was going to strangle my victim with the rope, but if they fought back I might need a knife. Plus, a switch-blade would lend the whole event a ceremonial feel.

I hid it in my bag and threaded my way through the crowds. As I walked I couldn't resist the temptation to slip my hand back into my bag and push the button. Click, it flipped out; click, back in. It made me feel dizzy. I'm the Angel of Death. I could kill any one of these people. The way I saw it, those who get killed are the ones who are worth the effort. These people weren't right. The spindly man walking towards me, combing his hair? No, he wasn't right. None of them were right.

Back at home I used the pliers to pinch hold of the broken-off key, but no matter how hard I tugged and yanked, it just wouldn't budge. After an hour, I was furious and began attacking the safe with the pliers instead, until the bit between my thumb and forefinger started throbbing and tears started rolling down my cheeks. I had to keep at it. I couldn't go through with it without money.

At 1.30 the neighbour's door banged shut. It was Old He, heading out. Things may not have been going well, but my plan wasn't ruined yet. I grabbed my bag and opened the door. I was going to follow him.

Mr He had a worn-out hunting dog who walked by lifting his legs in a languid, funny way, like a dignified mare. Every once in a while they stopped, Mr He to scratch his arm while the animal smeared his flea-infested back all over his master's leg. He lay down periodically, refusing to continue, to which the old man responded with a gob full of phlegm and a kick to his stomach: 'Useless dog, hurry up and die.' He snorted a response and Mr He whipped the sorry mutt with his leather belt before he pulled himself up onto his unsteady feet. Mr He had to keep throwing biscuit crumbs onto the road ahead just to get him to walk on.

I understood the guy's particular kind of loneliness. He was used to being someone important in the military academy, looking down on people. It wasn't death that scared him, more like the way time seemed to stretch out endlessly. He hardly slept. He was up early every morning walking the dog, coming back as the sun rose, when he would make a big fuss over breakfast. Then he would walk to the sentry box to collect the newspaper, which he read fastidiously all morning, taking in each and every word before launching into the operation that was lunch. Then came the hour-long nap and another walk with the old dog. Mr He wasn't a nice guy, no nicer than my aunt, but he wasn't the right victim either.

I couldn't be bothered to follow him any more so I went home, shoved some soapy water in the lock and had another go with the pliers. I stood there, anger rising up in me like steam building in a bottle, slowly expanding and pressing against me until I exploded under the pressure. Gripping the pliers, I attacked the lock, but it fought back.

I lay down on the bed and tried to calm myself, but panic gripped me. I got up and lay back down again, repeating the cycle, each time thinking I'd come up with a solution, only to descend deeper into my anxiety. The last time I got up I felt so impotent, all I could think of was how much I wanted to punish it. So I pissed into the lock. Then I grabbed the base, hunched one shoulder up like a bull, roared three times and turned it upside down. It crashed to the floor. It was too much to hope that the force might've popped it open, but I did notice that the underside had a plastic bag glued tightly across it. I ripped away the bag and found some bubble wrap and old newspapers, inside which was a round, flat piece of jade carved with the image of a Buddha. It was shiny like a mirror. The room was dark, so I went to find some light and watched as the Buddha danced under the rays. He laughed with his mouth, eyes and eyebrows. Even the red birthmark on his temple was laughing – laughing so that the rolls of fat and robes covering them were billowing like waves.

I too laughed, laughed so that tears gathered in my eyes. I wanted to pick up the phone and tell someone, anyone, about how I'd managed at least to unlock the strange mind of my petty aunt and her secret hiding place. She'd been almost stupidly clever. She didn't trust anyone, not even herself. She believed the most dangerous place to be the safest. She'd stuck her most precious possession on the *bottom* of the safe.

Just then Old He returned and I checked the time on my mobile: 6.30 – dinnertime exactly. That's right, fucking army guy.

Build-up

The next morning I went to the market and wandered around for some time before picking out a shopkeeper who looked as if he might know a thing or two about antiques. He had a bony face and white hair and he peered out from behind a pair of thick glasses. I decided that if he gave me a reasonable price I'd just take it and leave. But he examined the Buddha without saying anything. I asked him how much it was worth and he um-ed and ah-ed, started to utter something and swallowed it. He looked at me uncomfortably. I kept pushing him until he spoke.

'Young man, how much do you think it's worth?'

'I'm asking you. You're the expert.'

He traced the Buddha's outline with his thumb. 'Yes it's made out of jade, but it's a bit cloudy.'

'What do you think?'

'Five hundred.'

I took the Buddha back. 'Five hundred? Go buy yourself some instant noodles.'

'Then how much do you think it's worth?'

'Ten thousand.'

'What!'

'Watch me sell it for twenty thousand if you don't believe me.'

He laughed. 'You're a funny young man.' He was mocking me, so I started to walk off until I heard him call out after me: 'Three thousand. Let's be serious. Three thousand is a reasonable price.'

'Ten thousand.'

He muttered again to himself before offering five. I looked the old guy straight in the eye and enunciated, 'Fifteen.'

'There you go, you started with ten thousand and now you want fifteen.'

'Twenty thousand.'

He flapped his hands helplessly. I heard him muttering behind me and organising his thoughts, so I walked outside and hid behind a tree, from where I could see his shop door. Within seconds he popped his head out like a little mouse and looked around him. He spotted me and started waving his hands wildly.

'You! Come over here!'

'You want to buy it?'

'Yes, for ten thousand.'

'What do you take me for?'

I walked off. I was playing hardball, but if I'm honest I had no idea how much it was worth. If he didn't come after me it would be no big deal. I'd just go back. I had thick skin. But I could tell from the way he was acting that it was worth some serious dosh. The old guy was running after me, clanking like a rusty bike chain. He couldn't catch up and I was only walking, so I stopped.

'If you're serious, go get the money. I'll wait for you here.'

He ran back, leaving his dignity behind him. He stopped at the door and looked round to check that I was still waiting. An obscene smile spread across his face and he held up one finger. I made a show of putting together my thumb and index finger. *Got it.*

After returning with the money, he wanted to check the jade Buddha again to be sure I hadn't swapped it for another one. Then he handed me a bundle of notes. Ten thousand. I pushed it back and he held out another bundle. I stuffed one bundle in my bag and the other in my pocket.

'You're not going to count it?' he asked.

'It's all there. You're just worried I'm going to change my mind.'

At that moment a beggar came shuffling up to us carrying a metal bowl. I peered in, only five- and ten-cent coins. I unceremoniously dumped one of the ten thousand *yuan* bundles into his bowl. The beggar looked up at me and his neck stiffened. It seemed for a moment as if he was going to cry, but no tears came so I kicked him, which seemed to jolt him awake. He dropped his stick and disappeared like the wind. The shopkeeper was stunned. He must have realised I didn't give a shit how much the Buddha was worth. I only needed ten thousand.

I ate lunch. Deciding to save a few cents, I then took the bus to the train station.

The square in front of the station was hemmed in by a wall on one side, upon which was painted a gigantic map of China. People passed before it like swelling, pulsing shoals of fish. I joined them, standing in front as if standing before the river of time. Tomorrow the Chief of Police might be standing here too. He'd ponder the very same question I was pondering right there and then: where would someone go if they were on the run? To me, this was a question with endless possible answers. The Chief of Police would cut the map in two according to two fundamental possible choices: the first, places of emotional resonance; the second, places with people known to the fugitive.

I thought for a bit and realised I didn't have a strong emotional connection to a single person in the whole wide world. There was my cousin, I guess, on my father's side. But the only person I really felt a bond with was myself. For ages I'd dreamed of climbing some famous mountain and watching the sun rise. Indeed, for a while I believed it to be the only way to cure an exhausted heart.

I went to the ticket hall and started queuing. I was going to buy a ticket for the next day, 4.30 in the afternoon. After standing in the queue for half an hour I realised that the train would only be passing through this station, so there was a chance it could be delayed. I left the queue to think through my options again. I ended up buying a ticket for a train that left the next day at 4.10 because it originated in the city. After that I found an airline ticket office far from the station and called them. I used the video function to show them my ID and bought myself a discounted ticket for a few hundred, leaving at 9.00 in the evening the next day.

In the afternoon I went back to the clothes shop. The owner was wearing an old skirt suit and was taking a nap with her head on the counter. Dribble was leaching from the corner of her mouth and her eyes weren't fully closed, revealing a ghastly white cleft. The doorbell tinkled as I entered. The shirt, suit, leather shoes and briefcase I'd tried on last time were dumped in a pile and still hadn't been put away.

I knocked on the counter, bringing her back from distant dreamlands.

'Anything caught your fancy?'

I pointed to the four items. She looked at them, looked at me and then it came back to her.

'But I offered them to you for two hundred and you didn't want them.'

'No, I want them. Two sets.'

I peeled four notes from the bundle of money. She eyed them suspiciously until a smile suddenly opened across her face like an umbrella and she sprang into action. I felt like God sprinkling sweet nectar on this wretched woman.

She poured me tea and kept saying, 'I knew you were a decent young man.'

I figured that if I gave her a list she could source the stuff for me from other shops if she didn't have them: a leather belt, shoe polish, cologne, a hat and the rest of the half-used bottle of hair gel – for free, of course. I got her to swap the hat for a bigger one.

After she'd put the stuff in a bag, she rubbed her hands together like a child waiting for her reward. I took out another two hundred.

'Thank you, Uncle,' she said. 'Uncle must be a very important man.'

I also bought some rat poison, a couple of packets of crackers and water to take care of Old He's dog. I ripped open and polished off one packet as soon as I got back home. Then I poured rat poison onto another packet of crackers, bashing the plastic bag until they were broken into crumbs. After that was done, I started packing excitedly as if I was just a normal tourist off on holiday. I stuffed the money deep into the bottom of my bag and filled it up with underpants, shoe polish, a toothbrush, toothpaste, a towel, shampoo, soap, more crackers and water, then I placed the glasses, briefcase, shirts, suits, socks, the leather belt, leather shoes, hair gel, a comb and the bottle of cologne on top of those. I slipped the train tickets and two ID cards into my wallet. One of them was fake. I got it before I could grow a beard just for a bit of a laugh. It cost me one hundred *yuan* from a guy who specialised in fake documents. Say hello to Li Ming, from Beijing.

I grabbed the hat and kneaded it before putting it on. Then I checked to see that I hadn't forgotten anything. I didn't trust myself, so I opened my bag and tipped everything out. Turns out I was right to, as I'd forgotten to pack a razor. Not that forgetting a razor was a fatal error or anything – I could've just bought one downstairs. But it reminded me that this was one of the last things over which I would have total control and responsibility. If they caught me, that is.

After that I started tidying up the flat. The living room was small and when my aunt was here she'd stuffed it with all sorts of useless objects. I closed the windows on two sides, pulled the curtains across and started pushing the TV table, sofa, shoe rack and bonsai into one corner. Then I mopped the floor clean and went to the bathroom to get to the washing machine. I pushed it out and placed it close to the door. I put the switchblade and rope in another corner of the room. I found the end of the duct tape and stuck the roll to the wall.

I lay down on the floor, doused myself in the last remains of my anxiety and called my mother. This was the first time I'd ever picked up the phone and called her of my own volition. We were always fighting.

When Pa died, Ma didn't shed a single tear. She just launched herself into her business selling fizzy drinks and snacks. She was stingy, my ma, preferring to drink only boiled water and do all her own heavy lifting. If I tried to eat any of her stock she'd bat me away, saying it was unhygienic, that they'd all been fried in second-hand oil. I'd retort that such famous brands couldn't possibly endanger their customers' health in such a way and she had to admit that it was also a question of lost profit.

'Why do you care so much about making money?' I asked.

'For you, of course.'

'For me? And yet I'm not allowed to eat even one packet?'

'I'm trying my best to scrape together a living. For you, yes.'

'And what if I get cancer? Won't it all have been for nothing?'

'Well, you're not having it anyway,' she replied in her arbitrary way.

Money was her only love. Every cent that passed through my fingers made her eyes bulge in anguish. If she was forced to choose between me and one thousand *yuan*, well, you get the picture. Later I came to see it all differently. Those funny arguments only happened because she was scared to see me grow up, this illiterate woman whose one measure of life was the struggle to make money. It was her sole means of controlling me.

I argued with her less after that. She could do whatever she wanted. But now, as her voice reached out to me from the other end of the phone and I thought about the fact that I was about to leave this world for ever, tears welled up in my eyes. You only have one mother. I'd read that in a book. I sat up quietly and listened to her solemn counsel.

'Son, you've completed an important stage in your life, so make sure you listen to what your uncle and aunt tell you and work hard.'

'Mm,' came my reply.

We didn't have much to say to each other, so I asked, 'Has Auntie arrived?'

'Yes, she's here. She's very good to me. She brought me lots of expensive clothes.'

'When's she coming back?'

'Tomorrow afternoon.'

That was enough, so I hung up. Only one day left now. It was time. I decided to text Kong Jie. She was the only person I knew who would come over.

My aunt is driving me mad, I can't take it any more. I could kill her.

What is it? Calm down, we'll think of something, she replied.

Her voice was like a heavenly waterfall cascading over my body. Moments later it was gone. I hesitated. I could feel excitement in every bit of my body. I heard her voice again and it came clearly – soft, honest. Anxious. Loyal. It was the sound of love, even if I wasn't the only one to receive it. I burst into loud sobs.

I cried so hard it didn't feel real. I paced the room. I was miserable, because I knew now I would kill her. Because I could.

I found a notebook and wrote the date, but I couldn't think of anything to say so I jotted down some random sentences and then wrote:

it's her, it's her, it's her

it's her, it's her, it's her

But I tore that page out and burned it. I needed to leave this for the police. I started again:

cousin cousin cousin cousin

cousin cousin cousin cousin

I wrote page after page, until my hand hurt so much I had to stop.

Action

The alarm was set for 9.00 but I was awake by 8.00. I sent a text to Kong Jie.

We can't stand each other. I've nowhere to go. I'm packing my stuff and leaving this afternoon at 2.00. Can you come?

Can't you fix it? she replied.

No, I've already bought a train ticket back home for this evening.

There was nothing for a long time. I stared at the phone, my plan falling apart. Relationships never last. What's important to one person is just piffling dog shit to another.

Just then her reply bleeped onto the screen.

Don't be too hasty, see if you can fix things first?

Can we talk?

Sure, she replied.

I called her. 'Can you come, then?'

There was no sound on the other end. She didn't want to. She was nice to everyone, but I creeped her out. I was an inconvenience.

'Forget I said anything. It doesn't matter,' I said, and hung up.

After a while she sent a message.

I'll be there. Don't be upset. No matter how bad things get, they can always be fixed. Trust me.

Thanks.

My reply was deliberately cold. But I was relieved. She was coming.

Old Mr He was making a stir-fry next door; I could hear the metal spoon scraping the bottom of the wok. The sound made my teeth hurt. I took pleasure in knowing that his stupid mutt would soon be dead.

I changed into a T-shirt, put on my cap and went downstairs. It was nearly time for the guards to swap shift. I slapped my flip-flops against the tarmac so that they echoed. The guard looked at me sideways, his hands stuck firmly to the seams of his trousers and his body still, like a sculpture. I walked closer to get a better look. Sweat poured from his hat like rain from the eaves. His fingertips and buttocks were trembling from the strain.

I coughed a few times while I thought of something to say.

'Hey, buddy, are you on duty this afternoon?'

He turned his face ninety degrees like a robot to look at me and saluted.

'Yes, until 3.00.'

'I've got a friend coming at 2.00. Could you let them in?'

'What does he look like?'

'It's a girl.'

He smiled meaningfully.

I removed my cap and fanned myself. 'It's roasting,' I said.

'Sure is,' he said, taking a moment to relax.

He obviously wanted to chat, but I sauntered off. I loathed everything about his life. I wasn't going to become friends with him.

There were still a few more hours to kill, so I found a struggling barber's shop, walked in and announced, 'My hair's a mess. I want it sorted.'

They swooped like sparrows, switching on the electric fan, making tea, moving chairs. How did I want it washed? What style was I thinking of? I flicked through a magazine, but they were all hideous.

'Got anything more normal?'

They fetched another magazine filled with squeaky-clean Japanese and Korean youths. I gesticulated, trying to describe what I wanted, but I couldn't. At that moment an ageless news anchor appeared on the TV.

'Like that,' I said, pointing.

I stared at the TV and suddenly it occurred to me that the broadcaster's every movement, his every word, was a perfect display of his suitability for the job. I asked for pen and paper and started making notes. If you want to gain people's respect and trust quickly you have to adhere to the following principles:

1. Dress in clean, plain clothing in a palette of sombre colours.
2. Keep hair in a neat side-parting pushed back to the right. No hair must ever fall out of place. Wash it regularly to keep it looking healthy and shiny.
3. Don't be too expressive.
4. All movements should be sedate, natural and moderate.
5. Head should be kept upright, chin ever so slightly pulled back and a sincere smile should be adopted at all times.
6. Eyes shouldn't be too open, nor should they glaze over. They should be bright, mild and focused straight ahead (if angled slightly downwards). The person in front of you is always the most important person in the room.

I examined myself in the mirror, but the face staring back at me was the very opposite of this description. My eyes were cold and detached, the corners of my mouth were pulled downwards, my beard was stubbly, my hair pointed in all directions. Lethargy and boredom, which seemed to have grown in me over the years, were etched into my face. I may not have been a criminal yet, but I made a good suspect.

I tried imitating the broadcaster's demeanour, but it wasn't easy. Hardest to capture was his overall sense of decorum, and for a while the hairdresser and I found my attempt the funniest thing in the world. But my eyes lit up once the hairdresser was done. I almost didn't recognise the dignified man looking back at me.

It was still early, so I went to play pool. Being the middle of the morning, the place was empty, so I suggested to the boss that we play a game.

He looked at me sideways and then replied evenly, 'I don't really know how to play.' He was already holding a cue.

'Me neither.'

He fluffed the break, so I wanted to let him go again, but he said, 'Rules are rules. No special favours here.'

'OK,' I replied, took up my cue and bent over the table awkwardly to make my shot.

The first game was worth fifty, but I didn't want to win and he was unwilling to pot the balls.

'I'm rubbish,' he kept repeating.

I knew he was just bullshitting, waiting for the perfect moment to clear the table. Which he did, swiftly finishing this game and the next.

He wanted to raise the stake for the third game and I said fine.

'I want a proper game this time,' he said, to which I said fine again.

He knew the fight hadn't risen in me yet, so he continued his pretence, considering each shot carefully, aligning the cue and changing his mind, even though he could've made every single one.

I grabbed a beer from the fridge, bit off the cap and took a glug. I closed my eyes. To be honest, I was fed up. It was the same every time I played pool. I'd want to play at first, but by the third game all interest in it would've seeped out of me and my opponent would nag me more and more.

This guy wasn't making real shots, only trying to make mine more difficult. 'You're letting me win,' he said with an ingratiating smile.

I went to take a look. I knew he thought I wouldn't be able to pot anything, so I bounced the white off the cushion and sank a ball before clearing the table until only the black remained. He looked like a soldier about to be decapitated in battle and put his cue to one side, so I deliberately potted the white. It was his turn now.

'That was careless, brother.'

'Buy me a beer,' I said.

He wanted to play another game, not for money this time, but I shook my head.

'There's something I want to say, but I don't know if you'll understand. Even though you're older than me.'

'Try me.'

'Every time I play pool I get this nauseous feeling and I end up thinking I'd be better off dead.'

'I understand. I understand more than you do.'

Of course he understood. What on earth could be worse than spending your life running a pool shack, watching the balls being racked up and sunk, again and again. It was like Dostoevsky wrote in *The House of the Dead*: force a prisoner only to pour water from one bucket to another and then back again, within days they're contemplating suicide, or else how to get the death penalty.

For lunch I ate fried chicken wings, my Last Supper, and bought a cheap razor. Back at home, I waited and made sure everything was in place. I felt like a craftsman admiring his handiwork.

I closed my eyes and imagined a tangerine light, Kong Jie shaking her hair free, slipping off her silk skirt and curling up under the covers. As she stretches, pressing her lips together, skin pulled taut, her body rises and falls. And I'm like a soldier on a dawn raid, marching my gun through the rainy night. I'm coming, my body starting to explode open like fireworks, but I stretch it out, until the moment detonates completely. I think I might have more to come, but I don't.

I tore off a piece of toilet paper and wiped my sticky hands. I felt pretty gloomy. It was as if grey molecules were rising from the ground and falling from the sky at the same time, as if the whole world was drowning in them.

Afterwards all I could think was that the moment was approaching. I could hardly wait. I changed into another T-shirt and some tracksuit trousers, grabbed my switch-blade and started pacing.

She didn't understand, so I repeated, 'It's part of the plan.'

I watched as the tiniest sweat pearls ran down her arm, glittering and translucent. She looked like she was sculpted from glossy porcelain and she smelt of forest leaves after the rain. I stopped. She turned around and waited for me. In that long, lazy moment, she shielded her eyes with her hand and looked up at the sky. There wasn't a cloud above; the sky was a vast deep blue vault and the sun a ball of welding sparks. She bore her pearly teeth, that stupid smile, like someone not all there in the head. Then she carried on walking.

It was torture, but I swallowed it deep into my belly. I kept wanting to call out to her, *Get as far away from here as possible.*

Finally she reached the door.

'Is your aunt really that difficult to talk to?'

'It is what it is,' I said.

She pulled the door open, revealing the inky blackness inside.

'Why don't you open the curtains?'

I went in and switched on the light, then closed the metal outer and wooden inner doors behind me.

She faltered. 'Where is she?'

I grunted a 'mm' in reply and walked across to my bedroom, pulled the curtain aside and peeked in.

At 2.30 I caught sight of her talking to the guard. She was half an hour late and I'd begun to think she wasn't coming. Kong Jie saw me and started walking over. She'd tied her hair in a ponytail and she was wearing a bleached white T-shirt and a light blue skirt. A necklace made of crystals glinted around her neck and a small square watch encrusted with gemstones decorated her wrist, along with a set of red prayer beads wrapped around it three times. Her shoes were embroidered with the most delicate lotus flowers. Life for her was this neat and finely detailed. Her eyes were like black pearls, her face as if flushed with rouge, her lips almost transparent, her breasts pert. I was breathless, flustered. A painted maiden.

'I'm not late, am I?' she said.

'It doesn't matter,' I said.

It suddenly struck me with an incredible force that she was letting me kill her. It wasn't my decision to make. She was the one in charge, walking in front of me, leading me up the stairs towards her death.

'Why are you still wearing your cap?' she said.

'It's part of the plan,' I said.

Execution

'She's sleeping,' I said.

Why was I still bothering with this story?

She examined the room carefully, her eyes falling on the suitcase. Then she saw the washing machine.

'You're taking this back too?'

I nodded stiffly.

We carried on with our awkward conversation. It felt like I was never going to do it. That is, until the spring in the clock on the wall suddenly burst into action, a bullet piercing through my heart as the bell inside chimed three times in quick succession. I stumbled behind her and fumbled for her waist, covering her mouth and nostrils with my other hand.

Her quick breaths were fighting back. I dug my fingers firmly into her cheekbones. She tried pulling my hand away, gouging her nails into me. She kicked me like an obstinate foal refusing to be tamed. I never imagined she would be so strong and sweat ran from my every pore.

I whispered quickly into her ear, 'Be gentle, please. I'm begging you.'

Suddenly she stopped, softened. I pulled the tape from the wall and, using my teeth, ripped off a length of about six inches. She was in a daze. As the tape was about to close up her mouth and nostrils, she started pulling and tearing at it. She spat it out like she was spitting out fruit peel. She flapped and screamed. The sound was piercing. A gunshot drawing a perfect arc through the air on its way to the street outside and into someone else's heart. I imagined armed soldiers and concerned citizens would be at my door within moments. She tried to keep screaming, but I muffled her.

Then I took out my switchblade, flipped it open and stabbed her in the waist.

This was my first murder. My hands, just like my soul, seemed empty. It didn't feel like the knife was cutting through her, but rather that her squelchy, muddy flesh was swallowing it.

My thoughts were slipping. It was scary and I wanted to silence them, stop myself, but instead I wrapped the rope around her neck. I couldn't tell if I was doing it right. I went back to the knife and stabbed her three more times in the chest. The rancid smell of raw flesh rushed into the room in waves. I pushed her, twitching, towards the window and, using the knife, pulled aside one corner of the curtain.

The guard was standing a few paces from his post, listening carefully, unsure if he had really heard what he thought he had. Had the scream come from inside the compound? Was it human? He'd heard her. I watched as he reluctantly went back to his post and assumed his usual position.

My breathing was heavy. Kong Jie was sliding down in my arms, so I let her slip completely to the floor. Her mouth was open, her eyes bulging, her brow, eye sockets, the bridge of her nose, her cheekbones – these normally hidden parts of her face were all jutting out at me. Her T-shirt was now a bright crimson, red with added red, the stain fresh and angry like a peony. The largest peony I'd ever seen. It was horrifying.

I'd destroyed her. She was gone for ever. Like a big sheet of glass thrown from a high building, there was no way of bringing her back.

I squatted down and started scratching the knife across her face and stabbing all over her body. The blade snapped and blood spurted onto my face. Then I took her in my arms and put her head first into the top-loading washing machine before staggering to the bathroom. I glanced back at her legs sticking out of the top.

I took off my clothes, switched on the shower. Blood washed from my body in a river of red. I growled in a deep voice as I scrubbed, before catching sight in the mirror of what looked like a dark stain on the back of my shoulder. It made me shake. I divided my body into seven parts and I started cleaning methodically from the top down. But I stopped and emerged from the shower like a wandering ghost. I started searching in the pool of blood on my bedroom floor. I couldn't find it, so I went to the washing machine. There it was, her phone. It still had a signal. I tore the battery out and threw it away.

I went back to the shower and got dressed in my usual T-shirt and gym shorts. I slipped into a pair of trainers, shoved on my cap and swung my bag onto my back. I was ready. I looked back one last time, only to see that I'd left the rope and crackers in the corner of the room. I pulled the curtains across, checked there was no one outside, opened the door and left.

I sprinkled some of the cracker and rat poison mix along the road as I walked. That'd sort out the old dog. My hands were shaking so I threw the rest away.

The guard had his back to me, standing straight as always. I'd tied my laces very loose in the hope of making my shoes quieter when I walked. But as I got closer to him, my confidence was suddenly knocked out of me. What if the bloodstain on my back had started to spread? Had I checked before dressing? I couldn't remember and wanted to go back.

At that moment his right leg seemed to cramp and twitch. He lifted his shoe from the ground. Then I watched, wide-eyed, as he turned around. I was frozen to the spot, my legs shaking violently, and I heard an awful noise that could only have come from me (why wasn't I wearing trousers?). My lips trembled. I didn't know what to say. I was waiting for him to step down from his post and grab me. But as soon as he recognised me beneath my cap he greeted me with a warm smile. My lips twitched again as if there was something I desperately wanted to say, but instead I merely shook my head meekly.

'Are you all right?'

I nodded and continued walking over to him. Most likely he was lonely, had no one to share his secrets with.

As soon as I'd walked my body past the guard, my limbs relaxed and demanded that I run. There's nothing more painful than trying to control that kind of instinct. I lifted each foot stiffly before putting it back down again. One step at a time, I kept going onwards. Once far enough away, I tried going a bit faster, but I was still scared that he might see. I imagined him watching me walk away. He'd just started his shift so he hadn't seen the girl come in, otherwise he would have realised that the scream must have come from my place. After me like a rocket. Kick me to the ground. Twist my arm behind my back. Pin me down.

A taxi pulled up. I threw my suitcase into the boot and slid into the back, slamming the door shut behind me. Suddenly, I was paralysed.

The driver turned around. 'Where to?'

'The train station, quick,' I gasped.

The taxi slipped along street after street and up onto a trunk road, flying along like a motorboat on a wide stretch of water. I looked back a few times to make sure no one was following before removing the battery from my phone and throwing it, along with my cap, out of the car window.

Outside the light was more beautiful than any I'd ever seen and the people more kind and gentle. They were like innocent children running in a field of flowers, singing and dancing. I imagined shaving my beard at the train station, changing into my suit. The plan was working and soon my transformation would be complete.

On the Run I

I got to the station entrance with only a minute to spare before they would be closing the platform gates and in front of me was an endless line of army recruits waiting to go through the security checks to enter the station. I thought about cutting in, but decided against it. What was the point? The passengers would be passing through the gates like the last drops of sand in a funnel and the staff would be making their last checks, walking up and down the aisles, locking the doors.

When I was finally inside the station terminal, I pulled my suitcase through to the waiting room for confirmation that my plan was falling apart if nothing else. But the passengers were still sitting around, the train number was still hanging at the ticket gate. Then I became aware of the announcement blasting over the station loudspeakers.

Delayed. My train.

Fortune was smiling on me.

I dumped the T-shirt, shorts and shoes in the toilet and changed into my shirt and suit, fastening my belt and tying the laces of my leather shoes. I combed my hair and applied some gel, sprayed a few spurts of cologne and put on my glasses. With a slim leather document folder under my arm and my suitcase behind me, I made my way back to the waiting room. My shoulders kept slumping involuntarily and I tried ordering them to straighten up. I felt awkward. But then I caught sight of a middle-aged man watching me and I didn't feel so bad. In his eyes I was an educated young person with a steady job. We started chatting and he asked what I did for a living.

'I work for an IT firm,' came my reply. And I sounded convincing. He looked ready to give me his daughter's hand in marriage, if he had one.

The noise in the waiting room grew louder. I went in, patted the banister and looked as angry as the rest of them. We had to wait considerably longer for two members of staff to come striding down the corridor and open the gate. I rushed forward, but then turned back around. There was no need. There was no one there: no police, no security, not even anyone from the railways. I waited for the rest of the passengers to pass through before sauntering behind them, as if shepherding a flock of ducks along the corridor, down the steps and onto the platform. A green train lay in wait, breathing out an air of faraway freedom. I pretended to be reluctant to board and climbed up into the second carriage.

Everywhere people were standing on seats, shoving their luggage into the overhead racks, or else edging their way around each other carrying steaming cartons of instant noodles.

I waited for them to settle and walked down the corridor towards the three last rows of empty seats. In the middle of the carriage I passed a poor farmer, his brow covered in sweat, his hands shaking. His clothes were wet, as if he'd just washed them, and he leaned on his side, groaning. A young girl tried to give him a bottle of patchouli oil, but he grimaced and shook his head. He was probably dying. I sat down in the last row.

But the train didn't leave. The conductor retreated into her cubbyhole and locked herself in.

I wanted to go over to her and say, 'I was on time. What about you guys? Do you know how serious a delay like this is?'

After a while, the train began moving away noiselessly. Or at least I felt a breeze. But then I looked out and saw the train beside ours leave the station. An optical illusion. It felt like a knife twisting in my chest. Any second now, I was going to explode. Trapped. Like a man stubbornly pushing his cart through the mud as it rained.

The platform outside my window was empty, silent. If the police came to take me away, I decided, I'd shout,

'Thank you. Thank you railway department and thank you train!'

Kong Jie's mother must have contacted the police by now. School gets out at 5.00 and it was 6.00. The police would be able to trace Kong Jie to my place using satellites. I wish I'd never done it. I could have taken her mobile with me, dumped it somewhere. Why did I have to let the signal go cold at my house?

I tried to sit myself down and make myself believe, just as Kong Jie's mother would still be clinging to the picture of her daughter's upcoming graduation, that it didn't mean anything. She was probably out of battery or spending time with friends. 'That daughter of mine has just forgotten to call. But I'll give her a good talking-to when she gets home.'

I started counting. By the time I get to two hundred the train will have left, I said to myself. Six hundred. We were still at the same platform. Just as I had decided to get up and ask the steward if she could let me off the train, a long whistle broke the silence. I froze. Then pure joy, as if in that moment I'd become another person. The sun had nearly disappeared and the sky was turning a dark blue. Branches were retreating, houses receding, the moon was trailing behind us. The world was finally on the fucking move.

But suddenly I felt alarmed. I wasn't leaving, I was

cutting myself off. A forever goodbye.

So began my life on the run.

I fell asleep amid the train's clanging.

I'm walking towards the security check with dread like a stone in my stomach. The old policeman pats me down and tells me to go, impatience in his voice. I want to raise my arms and hoot, but I sense one of the other officers looking up at me. A pair of young eyes filled with a frightening sense of duty. Sweeping searchlights. They come to a stop on my back – ten more steps to safety – and I keep walking under the heat of his suspicion.

Until: 'You there! You're bleeding.'

Sirens start and I'm running and, with legs made of springs, I leap up and over the roof. I'm flying through the air. I've escaped, I think. I look back, but they're right behind me. They're not giving up that easily. I escape into an old building by the side of the road.

I wake to the sound of thumping. Shit. The train is starting to move. Shit, shit. Only as the faces of the strangers around me come into focus do I return to reality. I go to the toilet, but it's locked, so I walk down the corridor and smoke a cigarette. The train is like a fish gliding through dark waters. I'm having a bit of a poetic moment.

I go back to my seat. Then I see them, two police officers standing at the other end of the carriage. They are carrying card machines to check everyone's IDs. All these innocents, happily rooting around in their bags. I couldn't tell if this was routine or they were looking for something in particular. But I didn't have time to think. I turned and went back to the toilet. I could feel them looking at me. I bent over, held my stomach and started banging on the door.

'Hold on,' came the voice from inside.

I pretended to go looking for the toilet in the next carriage, but realised halfway that this was the last one. I sat in an empty seat and stared blankly ahead. Maybe I could hide under the seat. No, that was a stupid idea. After a while someone came staggering towards me. The farmer again. His shoulder kept banging against the seats and the walls of the carriage. He was looking for somewhere to be sick. He pulled at the toilet door and then continued onwards.

'Get back,' I hissed.

He looked at me. The corners of his mouth twitched.

'Go back. I mean it.' I was guarding my territory.

He seemed to think of something and stumbled in the direction from which he'd come.

Just then I heard the sound of the door unlocking. I rushed over and pushed past the young woman who was emerging, fastening her belt. We got caught in a bit of a tussle before I made it inside. I nudged the door shut with my shoulder and locked it three times to be sure. I'd wait for a half an hour until they'd passed on and left the train, but I could hear the sound of scuffling and hushed talking. The police had found me out. I'd made myself a trap, I realised. The lower half of the window was fastened shut. The top was open, revealing a crack of black sky. But try as I might, I couldn't pull it further open.

Furious knocking at the door. I didn't answer. Kicking.

'Get the fuck out.' It was an unmistakable order.

Something pounded inside me, wanting to burst out. It needed me to run, but I couldn't. I was going crazy. The yelling and cursing were getting louder. My breaking point came as he shouted about my mother's flabby pussy. This isn't how it is supposed to go, I thought. I killed someone, sure, but you don't know that. Why do you need to insult my ma? Say whatever you like about me, but what right do you have to insult my ma?

I wrenched at the lock and pulled open the door. He grabbed me by the collar. I tried to push him off, but he was stronger. He picked me up as if I was no more than a little bird and moved me aside. He then charged in and, without closing the door, pulled down his trousers and started shitting.

Out in the corridor I heard only the hum of the air-conditioning. I'd never smelt anything like it.

No one came to speak to me. I drew myself up, feeling somewhat disappointed, as if I'd left matters half finished. The other passengers were talking about the farmer; in his rush, he'd knocked one of the police officers to the floor.

The older officer punched him to the ground, held him down with his elbow and growled, 'I knew there was something not quite right about you.'

I understood. My heart was thumping, but my face was stiff like dead wood. I struggled to hold back the laughter. I needed to pee. Despite being in there all that time, I hadn't gone and now I was about to wet my pants.

Holding it in, I knocked on the door. No answer. I went over to the washbasins. There was no one around, so I started pissing. Once the stream started it wouldn't stop, two minutes, ten minutes. Still going. It was goddamn embarrassing.

On the Run II

The train drew in to the first stop and I, along with a stream of other passengers, disembarked. I crouched in the shade of a nearby planter. We waited ages before one of the railway staff came to announce that the train would be leaving soon. The stallholders packed up and left, the platform gates were locked shut and I went down onto the tracks. I walked through the inky night, my feet soon covered in shit, which was pretty humiliating. Luckily I only had to walk ten minutes before I came to some lights.

I was walking fast. It felt familiar, but as I approached and saw the street lights, the houses and signs and even the shadows, everything seemed to be made of sharp knives thrusting at me. A few young guys stopped their game of pool and stared at me, puzzled as to my sudden appearance in the darkness. An old man sat beside them, fanning himself. He smiled, his mouth empty of teeth (they're going to kill me, I thought, and he'll watch them, clapping). Moments later, I was surrounded by motorbikes. They spoke quickly in the local dialect and I saw a fierceness in their eyes that was impossible to misinterpret. They weren't waiting for my answer. I was pulled onto one of the bikes, driven around the town and relieved of fifty *yuan* along the way.

I walked into Benefit the People Guest House, bag in one hand. The place had originally been someone's private home and there was still an altar burning incense in the front room-turned-lobby. Bars blocked all the windows street level, the tiles on the floor were slippery and the blanket smelt foul. I wanted a room on the first floor. They noted down my fake ID, saw I was from Beijing and felt flattered. But when I wanted them to change the black and white TV, they slammed the door shut in my face. The screen was capable of broadcasting one white thread only. The curtains were ragged, the sheets were sallow, the pillows black and without pillowcases. A pair of flip-flops sat sadly on the bathroom floor, one of them broken.

I snapped the bolt shut across the door and walked over to the window. I looked out on an empty courtyard and an endless sky. I had no idea why I was here, of all places.

For the next few days I didn't leave the room, except to go downstairs to eat. The kitchen was in the courtyard surrounded by a low wall. One time, after I'd finished dinner, I smashed the shards of glass pressed into it. Then I positioned a ladder I found lying around under my window. I might have been taking precautions. Or maybe I was just bored.

I took to sleeping. Excessive sleep and masturbation. I could recite the contents of the police poster on the wall by heart. Eighty-five characters in total, including three exclamation marks. At one point I detected the stench of dead rat. I went looking for it and discovered a smelly sock soaking in washing detergent in the bathroom. I was like a noble animal disgusted by its own excrement and the loneliness I had myself created. I started weaving together what remained of my life. I splashed the floor with water, mopped it, knelt down and went over it again with a cloth. Then I took a bottle of shoe polish and shined my shoes, wrung out the cloth and buffed until I could see my own reflection by the moonlight in the leather.

I had found happiness in labour, but the feeling passed just as quickly as I had found it. My body was telling me something, giving me an order: go outside.

Outside exploded with fireworks like a never-ending festival, like there was still love out there for an adventurer. But as I drew close, all I saw was one breeze block after another, one electrical pole after another, one street after another, one face after another, at once familiar and utterly unrecognisable. Never a car accident, never a fight, not even the gentlest of arguments. I saw an internet café, but it wouldn't be easy to use my fake ID and I didn't want to risk using my real one. A sign flashed CINEMA, but as I approached all I saw was a heap of rubble and a small market of people selling scraps for a few cents. A nearby kiosk carried no recent newspapers, so I bought two yellowing copies of *Sports Weekly* and *Former News Weekly* and went back to the guest house to read them. It took me seven hours to read every single character contained within their pages.

The second time I went out my hopeful mood was extinguished even faster. Before long, the order came again: go back. At that moment I understood like no one else in this world the torture that was old Mr He's existence. In winter he dreams of summer, in summer he misses winter; when he's out he wants to be back home, when home all he can think about is going out. But it's all the same, everywhere. That's why the old widower subjected himself to such a demanding regimen, as a distraction from his pathetic life.

We're both the lowest forms of trash, me and him, a fate from which we can't escape. Every day we long for the planes in the sky to throw out a rope and pull us up, to take us away somewhere more fulfilling. Even if where they take us affords us no freedom. But there are no such things as miracles, so instead we must endure this aching passage of time.

The second time I went out I bought a pair of

binoculars. I sat on the roof and looked out on the town. I saw people washing dishes in their kitchens, someone sitting on their bed mending the soles of their shoes, the final scenes before the curtains were drawn and the lights turned off. I went back to my fetid room and scrabbled around for my mobile phone, the last thing that could give away my whereabouts, the whore that had been seducing me ever since I went on the run.

I stopped myself.

I didn't switch it on.

I made for People's Park the next day. It has a mound like a golf course, dotted with groves of trees and the gravestones of martyrs. They'd carved out a lake in front of the hill and a pavilion had been put in the middle, connected to the square on the other side by a white marble bridge. Water spat like the strings of a harp. Medicinal herbs had been left to dry on the stones and a farmer's truck was parked in the distance, its back tyres missing, resting on a pile of planks. I was the only person in sight.

I approached the steps leading to the martyrs' graveyard, replaced the battery in my mobile and turned it on. The reception was crap and it took until I reached the top before 'new message' pinged on the screen. I felt a flash of hope and opened it.

Dear Sir/Madam, My name is Zhang Bing of Happiness

Boulevard Real Estate. Please feel free to contact me with all your real estate needs. Thank you!

Not a chirrup. No rustle of leaves. Rays of sunlight poked through the trees and laid themselves out, motionless, across the gravel path.

I remembered a short story I once read: the author, desolate and lonely, walked through a cemetery. Just as they were about to cover a coffin, he stopped to listen. What if someone was calling him? But there was only silence. That's how I felt at that moment. I wanted to sit and wait for the police. I was going to be executed and I had nothing left to say. Nothing to explain. But I ran away, crying. I chucked the battery, fled down the steps of the martyrs' graveyard and chased down a three-wheeled cart.

I looked back at the park through the binoculars from a hill in the distance. The lake, the square and the shimmering branches. A man emptying the bins. The next few glimpses were the same. I took a nap in the fading light. When I woke I reached straight for the binoculars. Rushing cars, crowds of people. I could feel their anger even from this far away. Their eyes were like flames sweeping across the park. They shook sticks as if waiting for me to come running out. A police dog pulled its masters, panting and dribbling, like a horse yanking on its reins. The officers followed behind it as it sniffed.

Before long they'd covered the entire park.

I stood up and ran down the hill. My feet pedalled hard against the ground, my teeth clattered, my brain rattled in my skull. Once at the bottom, I hailed another three-wheeler and told him to take me to Benefit the People Guest House, quick. I paid before we got there, but just as he was about to stop I told him to keep driving. I'd spotted a white van was parked out front. I'd never seen it parked there before.

'Where you going, kid?' the driver said.

I wasn't about to argue, so I told him to swing by a public toilet and ducked inside, from where I watched the door to the hostel. After a while, two puffy crimson-cheeked guys emerged, picking at their teeth. They sauntered towards the car, pulled up the windows, switched on the air-con and waited a while before driving off. I checked there was no one else around and approached the hostel. The lobby was empty, the only movement coming from papers fluttering on the desk, blown by the air-con. They couldn't have been gone long. I made for the stairs, walked down a corridor, unlocked a door, went in, closed it and pulled across the bolt. All without making the slightest sound. I threw my mobile and binoculars into my bag, swung it onto my back and stood in front of the door. It was so dark and quiet outside that it creeped me out. I didn't move. But before long I heard the sound of a man's footsteps. They were slow, yet purposeful. He was approaching the top of the stairs. I expected him to carry on up, but he paused on the landing before starting down the corridor towards me. Maybe he was staying in the next room. The footsteps disappeared. I waited for him to open the door, but there was only silence.

I took a step back and saw the shadow of two feet in the crack beneath the door. A man wearing a pair of enormous leather shoes was standing on the other side. I felt my breathing stop. Then, as if a gust of air had taken him, his shadow disappeared. He sure was patient.

After a short time a thudding came up the stairs.

'What's taken you so long?'

'Didn't I tell you keep a watch downstairs?' the first man hissed.

'Watch for what?' The second man trundled towards us. Then came a thumping on the door and the knocking hammered into my heart. 'No one's in,' he snarled.

'How do you know? Have you opened the door and looked?' the first guy said.

'Get the fuck out here!'

The second man started kicking the door as if he was stamping on it. The screws that secured the lock to the doorframe began to loosen. I moved – the place was suffocating, I was about to explode – and opened the window. I was panting hard. The yard at the back was empty, apart from the particles of dirt on the ground illuminated by the sun.

I swung my bag onto my back, climbed out onto the windowsill and felt my way onto the ladder. I wanted to get down quickly, but my legs felt unsteady. They would probably be waiting for me at the bottom. But they weren't and I didn't see them in the lobby either. I threw my bag over the wall and started scrambling up.

I looked back and saw two eyes as big as a bull's staring at me. It was the chef. His arms hung by his sides, his mouth opening and closing as he searched his thoughts. I could hear the door being blasted open upstairs.

'Shhh!' I said, feeling something in my pocket.

He looked scared. I jumped down and tried to stuff the two hundred *yuan* from my pocket into his hand. He looked down at the money, shook his head, but I grabbed his hand and pressed his palm shut. I then pushed him away. I thought he was going to cry, but he retreated into the kitchen.

I jumped over the wall, picked up my bag, threw it onto my back and ran into the bushes.

On the Run III

The car's headlights swept across the sky like the Monkey King's golden staff, a wolfhound howled and the city's dogs replied. Everything went quiet and all that was left was the sound of croaking toads. I curled up under a pile of corrugated asbestos tiles behind the duck pond and watched as the last people left.

The lights of the town shone in the distance as I walked around the mountain. Where there was no footpath I followed the main road, making my way back to the foot of the slope. I walked for hours, as if lost, until I came to a river. The water's gurgling calmed me. I untied a petrol drum and with great effort rowed it downstream. Tired, I realised I didn't have to row it and instead I floated in the darkness, deep into the belly of the universe.

As dawn crept across the sky, I spotted a tidal bore spitting white bubbles like a swimmer churning through the water. The fishy smell of the day's first boat came next. I ate my breakfast, which roused my spirits, and felt my strength returning. A whistle sounded, beautiful, like a giant, his feet planted in the centre of the river, inhaling and letting out a sonorous cry. I went to buy a ticket and then took up my place on the deck, waiting for the waves to crash against the side of the boat and splash against my face. But I couldn't stop sleep from taking me. I copied the guys from *The Outlaws of Wulong Mountain* and lit a cigarette before drifting off to sleep so that I would wake as it burned my fingertips.

But I opened my eyes to find my hand empty. Dead to the world, I must have flicked the cigarette away in my dream. My bag was still wedged between my body and the deck's barrier. The rest of the passengers were similarly squeezed between luggage. The sun was high in the sky, melting us like in a furnace. I was grimy with oil and stank like hell.

I arrived, along with the boat, in a city that reeked of fish. Using my fake ID, I checked into a love motel and went to sleep with my shoes on, as if I was at home in my own bed. It was dark by the time I awoke. I'd probably only been asleep for a few hours, which the clerk confirmed when I checked out, as he charged me for four. So I made for the university to find a student room for the night. I felt safer there than in a hotel.

A few days later I bought a T-shirt, shorts and a massive cap much like the ones I'd worn before and took an illegal cab to the bridge over the Yangtze. There, I crossed into the next province. I told the driver to stop by the police station.

I walked in and charged my phone. A woman sat at the window, quietly stamping papers. With my eyes on my screen, I spoke.

'What time do you close?'

'At 5.00,' she said, without looking up.

I switched off my phone and went outside to find another taxi. Another illegal cab took me back to the bridge. I had twenty unread messages, all from Ma, all saying the same thing: *Son, come back and give yourself up.*

It was an obvious police tactic and I was indignant. She could have refused to let them use her phone. How could she betray her only flesh and blood? What kind of mother was she? Then it struck me that she might not have been forced, but had thought of it herself. She felt guilt towards the family of the girl and society as a whole. That's my mother all over.

I bought a ticket for the TV tower. As the lift rose higher, I saw the first neon lights going on in the town on the other side, car lights moving, starting and stopping. The details were fuzzy, so I got out my binoculars. They'd be looking for me down there, exhausted from chasing me. Maybe they'd stop and look up at the tower. *He's on the other side!* they'd realise. But it wasn't just a question of crossing the river. The county, city and provincial authorities would have to inform the local police, as well as coordinate with the relevant bodies on this side. Maybe they'd think it too much trouble and wait for the police back home to arrive. *This one's ours, guys.*

I wanted to get a boat to the next place, but then I thought, why run if they're not coming for me? So I stayed a few more days.

I got to know a spindly kid of twelve, his limbs like twigs. He wore baggy green army gear. I was eating some wonton at a place near my hostel at the time, when he approached looking anxious (I swear, looked as if he was about to die). His face twitched and he came running up as if moved by a gust of passing wind. I stood up to watch, but he pushed in behind me, pressed against the wall. Four young guys with leathery dark skin and fierce eyes came running in. They were covered in dragon tattoos and carried knives.

The hand clutching my T-shirt was shaking, I could feel it, but after a while he came out from behind me and sat down in front of me, this time with feigned confidence. I carried on eating my wonton, but I didn't feel too comfortable. He watched me like a mother watching a baby nestled at her bosom, or like a boy from the village looking at his older cousin from the city. It was intimate somehow.

'You still here?' I said.

'You're not from around here,' he said, and smiled, stroking my newly laundered white T-shirt. 'Nice stuff.'

I felt disgusted, so I got the bill and left. But he followed me.

'Go home,' I said.

He laughed.

'I'm busy. Don't follow me.'

He stopped. I started walking in the opposite direction to my hostel. But I couldn't stop thinking about him. Maybe he was an orphan? Maybe we could be brothers? Maybe he could help me out? But I told him to get lost.

The next day I went back to the same wonton place and again he appeared. We didn't think it was strange.

'I knew you'd come back,' he said.

He watched me eat. I looked out to the street and ordered him a bowl. But he kept watching me. It was as if I ate funny, not like the people from around here. It was something to see.

Once we'd finished he asked, 'Where to next?'

I didn't know what to say. He was a bad kid, but cute. We went to the market, where he stroked the water pistols, his eyes looking up at me. I made to leave, but he tugged on my T-shirt, kind of embarrassed, like a spoilt little girl. Until I got my wallet out. We bought a few things and then went to the arcade. He flew a plane, his right hand jiggling the joystick anxiously, his left occasionally slapping the machine, his eyes transfixed and unblinking. I played a few times and kept getting killed off. I said I wanted to go, but he ignored me. I repeated myself, but he continued exploding bombs, *pa-pa-pa*, before eventually tearing himself away.

Outside, a crowd had gathered around a noticeboard. I went to take a look. A new wanted poster had gone up, the face of a coarse middle-aged man with droopy eyes who'd killed seventeen people. In the corner beside it was a small poster, a side dish to his main course: a young man who'd murdered his classmate. He may have only had one victim, but he looked more creepy, his hair fluffy, his beard stubbly, dressed in a dirty T-shirt, biting his cheeks, his chin turned up. His expression was detached, yet provocative. It was the first time I'd seen myself in three weeks.

HE WAS DRESSED IN FLIP-FLOPS AND GYM SHORTS AT THE TIME OF HIS DISAPPEARANCE.

I was worth fifty thousand.

'Hey, he looks like you,' the kid said with excitement, as if he'd just discovered the secret connection between all living things.

I patted him on the back of the head, batting him away. Having eaten, we went our separate ways. But I didn't go far before turning around and, with darkness as my cover, following him. He seemed to be ruminating as he walked, until suddenly he laughed. He came to a slope, jumped down onto the half-finished road and climbed through an open window. The heaps of soil on either side were covered in weeds that were almost as tall as the old house. I climbed down onto the rooftop, moved some of the tiles and peered through the small crack.

A decrepit old man sat in a large armchair with his feet placed in a bucket of cold water. His eyes were closed. He held an old radio to his ear and was tuning the stations, pulling occasionally on the aerial. A cat lay quietly on the table. When the kid approached, it flew off and found another place to lie back down. He didn't make a noise, but he had a definite swagger. He strode around with his hands on his hips, occasionally knocking himself on the head in frustration.

The kid then went to the cupboard and pulled out a leather suitcase. He moved the lamp to the table and started fiddling with a long piece of wire. He had his head cocked, just like me, listening. His shadow reached out across the floor. He went to the kitchen and emerged with a spoonful of oil and carefully poured it into the lock. Then in went the wire again. Before long, the lock pinged open. Instead of looking over at the old man, he looked straight up at me. He seemed nervous. I froze and was going to pull back, but then I thought, if he's seen me, he's already seen me. So I continued to watch. He removed a bag tied with a rubber band and in it found a bunch of notes. He licked his fingers and counted. Then he put the stool up against the window. I was still lying on the roof. I waited for him to climb out and disappear into the night.

But instead he climbed back in. He went for the cat and, as if they were intimate friends, he took hold of it, cuddling it in his arms. He then took something from his pocket. Food, I thought. The cat closed its eyes and yawned, as if human in that moment. But it was a rope. The kid tied it around the cat's neck. Then he tugged, pulling the two ends in opposite directions, strangling it. The cat's mouth opened, its cries became a thick panting that floated on the air. He pulled the cat up so that it was standing, just to make sure it was really dead. Its back legs reached for the boy's thighs. It scratched, like a mouse running in mid-air. Its fur was spiky. By the time the boy let go, exhausted, the cat was stiff like wood.

He was dripping with sweat, but he carefully placed the cat on the old man's knee. He then climbed out and jogged away. I wanted to be sick. The old man was still listening to the radio, stroking his furry companion whenever they said something funny.

I decided I had to leave this city.

When I left my room the next day the kid was there, waiting for me.

'How did you know where I was staying?' I stuttered.

'I followed you the first day we met.'

He smiled and I felt sick, my hairs standing on end. I decided not to collect the deposit but just take my bag and leave. But he grabbed my sleeve.

'I've got no one else to play with. You're a good guy. No one else pays me any attention.'

I brushed him off, but he pulled harder as tears and laughter fought against each other on his face. I hit him and he let go, wounded.

'I knew you'd leave.'

The intimacy of his words knocked me dull and I watched him disappear.

As he walked through the gate, I called down to him. He turned and answered. I motioned for him to speak first.

'Brother, I know who you are.'

'How much do you want?'

'I've got money. I made a few *yuan* last night.'

'Then go and have fun, don't mind me.'

'I want to buy you something. Guys like you on TV always wear a tie. I came to ask if you like red.'

'There's no need.'

'I have to give it to you. Don't go.'

He watched me as he retreated, afraid I'd leave. He then turned and ran. I went back to my room and got my bag. By the time I was on the street, he had gone.

I walked for a bit and hid in the shade of a tree. But real brotherhood wasn't easy to find these days, so I took out my binoculars to look for him. People walked back and forth, forming a moving barrier. I couldn't see him. I was about to put the binoculars away when the kid hurried into view with three large policemen. They were waiting at a pedestrian crossing. The kid walked with care, smearing his hands on his dirty army uniform. He look looked up at the policemen and chatted. Shameless.

My hands shook and drops of sweat ran across me like hungry mice. I watched his animated expression as he pointed in my direction and I felt I was sinking into the ground beneath me, while the boy, a god, placed a curse upon my head. One of the policemen was tapping at his cheek with his index finger. He looked over and then started waving. The two other policemen took up the flank and charged straight towards me. Only then, as the reality that I was about to be caught hit me, did I know to put away my binoculars, sling the bag on my back, tighten the straps and run for my life.

My legs thudded against ground. They felt powerless and far too heavy. It was like running on cotton wool, or through deep water. But I kept running. Behind me: 'Wait! Stop!' They were flustered. I heard the panting. I was running in the hundred-metre finals at the Olympics: my arms made a scissor motion, my head pecked through the air. People kept stopping to watch. I was the wind against their cheeks.

The police stopped and gasped, 'Stop or we'll shoot!'

Go on, then. I was already at one with time and matter, my body running for the sake of running.

I ran at the edge of time itself. Time had to me always felt sticky; the past was the present, the present was the future, yesterday, today and tomorrow were one boundless, mashed-up whole. But now it was an arrow shooting out in front, a point out from which it fired. It was bright, brave, fearless. In the diabolical light of the sun, it pierced through all possible futures, burned up into a black slag heap of the past. I would run, I would crush it. It smelt like a cow condensed into one piece of beef jerky, every bead of sweat suspended in the air collected into one.

A black car crashed and crumpled into pieces like a mirage. It was spluttering like all old cars, old and shabby, as if it could fall apart at any moment and reveal its wounds on the street right there. But it came out of nowhere, came hurtling towards me from a distance. Six seconds. I was forced into a side alley. Interfering busybodies. A swarm of scooters followed me. They smiled covertly at the police, ready to be heroes, but they were pathetic. They forced me to throw coal scuttles, beer bottles, broken chairs and even prams that may or may not have contained children. Every few steps a wooden door was flung open, warm looks of concern, promises of old wardrobes, hidden cubbyholes, secret tunnels, invitations in. But I'd rather die right there on the street.

I trusted no one, not since that dream on the train.

That afternoon, I ran through a labyrinth of alleyways. I remember silence, sunlight through the eaves and spread across walls, my shadow brushing past. It was as surreal as a film. Those scooters (masterpieces of modern machinery) were about to kick their hooves and sink their teeth and claws into my arse.

I stopped suddenly. As if God had spoken to me. I slipped into a dark corner. A motorbike came driving towards me, ridden by a smart-looking cop. He came through the narrow passage as if he was on an open road. A siren followed. I waited for the whirlwind to break on top of me, then rushed forward and pushed. The bike veered towards the wall like a decapitated dragon. Its front wheel chomped through a pile of bricks before coming to a halt. The body of the bike spun one hundred and eighty. The policeman fell like a sack of cement and there he lay by the wall, battered and flattened, until the bike grew bored and spun aside. He sat up, brushed away the dirt and tried to get up. But his eyes rolled back and he slumped. A drop of water fell from the sky and cracked in front of him. He closed his eyes. His chest heaved. People came rushing out.

'Someone went running that way. Quick!' I said.

I walked away briskly, then spotted an unlocked bike. I rode furiously towards the market, threading through the crowd and into a busy grocery shop. From inside I spotted a taxi. I pulled open the back door.

'Where to?' the driver asked.

I took out my phone and secretly pressed it between the cushions in the back seat. I made my excuses and got out. I waited for the taxi to pull away and then started in the direction of the train station freight yard.

I followed the path by the tracks, my back to the station. They would close all roads, but they wouldn't think of the train tracks. That that's how criminals like me escape. Right now they'd be asking themselves a stupid question: save their colleague or go after me?

Suddenly, I felt all grown up.

The Ending

Being on the run is like playing a game of hide-and-seek. I'd knock on doors and run away, then they'd come running after, a wildness in their eyes. But I'd leave them in the middle of nowhere. I lost a shoe in my escape. Until the day I saw the sign for T— City. I stopped short, numb. So this had been my destination all along, the day I killed Kong Jie and boarded the train. This was where my cousin lived. I thought I'd been moving without a plan, but my subconscious had been drawing me here. I was so tired I could barely control myself, like an ox after a day toiling in the fields that in the distance makes out the outline of the village.

I caught a bus to the outskirts of town and then scrabbled across a small mountain covered in scrub and trees. In the distance, a winding road cut across the plain. Every now and again a vehicle would speed along it like a ghost. To the west sat an orphaned house. My cousin's marital home, one floor had now become two. But they had yet to clad the top storey with the requisite ceramic tiles. I could see the dark red bricks and the aluminium windows set into them. A melon shack stood beside the road and four bare-chested, rugged men sat playing poker. They looked like plain-clothes policemen to me. The first one cooled himself with an electric fan, drawing electricity from the shack. Another bore his back, pink and delicate.

The door to the house was pulled shut and no one seemed to be at home. I waited until midday, when smoke started puffing from the chimney. Insects began hopping like tightly wound springs. I felt cut off, as if I was hanging from one of the beams, my mouth taped shut, watching as my family sat round the table at dinner, talking.

Knowing I could die at any moment, I had to see her.

She hadn't changed since the last time I was here to attend her wedding: two puckered hard pears for breasts, a body shrivelled and legs crooked with rickets. She walked us along this road to say goodbye, turned back for one last look, a wave, her eyes filled with tears. Her wave slowed, before resting in mid-air. A forever goodbye. But she came back when Pa died, with Auntie on her arm. Auntie's cancer was worse than Pa's, but she held on to life more firmly. With her white hair and determined expression, she would never surrender. My cousin cried until her eyes were puffy like peaches.

I didn't know what to do at the funeral, but I was pushed up on stage against my will. I should cry, I knew this, but my eyes were dry. Ma and Uncle were the same. Uncle sat by the coffin, smoking cigarette after cigarette (he would later quit, when we realised the smoking caused his cancer). Ma seemed to waver, her steps heavy. The other women in the family were embarrassed to cry when they saw her. The funeral was an obligation. Once my cousin led away the heft that was my auntie and the spattering of fireworks had been let off, the guard of honour made its way from the bridge. Only then did I let the tears come.

I watched the funeral procession approach. Pa was gone. My one and only pa, dead. My cousin dried her silent tears, tucked my head into her armpit and protected me. She held away that place, those people, the black night. Her eyes were heavy. She looked at me as if she was my mother, as if I was now an orphan, her tears frothy.

I wanted to see her.

I waited for the men by the melon shack to switch off the fan and leave in a minivan before coming down from my vantage point. That's when I saw her, carrying a large bundle of hay. She had her back towards me, her head bent low. She was out making hay. Fields to both sides of the house were planted with it and one section by the road had already been harvested. Insects leapt in the ploughed mud and a gust of wind sent the shiny leaves swirling. It was so quiet I felt a shiver go through me. My cousin worked quickly: one swish and the grass landed in her basket, then another. She was lost in the rhythm.

I heard my hesitant footsteps in the sandy dirt.

She was bait. All living things were prophets at that moment, watching me in amazement, as if I was walking step by step into a trap. I approached halfway, but stopped. A pulse of cold energy shot up my back. At that moment, she seemed to feel something, as she stopped cutting and slowly turned around.

'Who are you?' she managed to ask. She opened her mouth to scream, but it was as if she was paralysed. She could make no sound. Trembling, she retreated and grabbed hold of a bundle of hay by the high table behind her.

I watched her brandish the dry stalks as a weapon. It was pathetic, but nothing could be more hurtful. I reached out, my fingers spread, and walked towards her, but she was petrified. I didn't know it would turn out like this.

Then I understood, I understood it all. I wasn't going to stay here, where I wasn't wanted. I waved.

'I was just going to ask for some water.'

I'd drink and leave.

It was a predicament for her. She didn't move. The

sun was hot and illuminated her wrinkles and clumsily applied make-up, which looked threaded and bobbly. Her chest was extravagantly displayed (like two plates), her jeans barely able to contain her hips, the seams popping, her yellowed calves and ankles showing. She was a middle-aged woman gone sour.

'I'll leave as soon as I've had something to drink. I won't bother you.'

She looked sideways, her lips trembling. At first I thought she was scared, but then I realised she was mouthing something. Her freshly painted lips were speaking.

'Run. Quick.'

It was a painful reminder of my current reality, but I turned and ran. I slid on the gravelled surface and, almost falling over, ran up onto the main road. I heard the sound of a thousand safety catches being pulled back and a growling pack of wolfhounds (their breath stank). A car was approaching.

I nearly choked on the thick stench of petrol.

I tried moving my legs clumsily, hopelessly, and collapsed against a slope at the side of the road. Lights flashed across my crazed mind. But the car came screaming towards me, a speeding box in my vision. As if it was the one trying to escape.

The road was empty. Not a soul. Not a living

creature. No sirens in the distance. The sun caught on the tarmac, as if glimmering on the tops of lethargic waves. I looked into the distance: the door of the house was already firmly shut, blinds pulled down. The hay in the fields danced in the wind. She had become fat, wrinkled and a mother; she was a woman of small riches who put everything into pleasing her husband, cooing over him as if she owed him, cooking for him, earning money to give to him. And I was a devil who had disturbed her peaceful existence.

I climbed back up the slope and watched. Hours later, a man with a round ball for a belly and puffy lips hobbled into view. He was calling her name. She opened the door with trepidation, looked at him and suddenly took him into her arms. He clapped her on the back; tears rolled from her eyes and bubbles formed in her nostrils. He then released her, lunged and with a *pa!* he clapped his hands together, reaching his left hand out and his right up into the air before bringing it back down in a beheading motion. She laughed. The move had taken her by surprise and she stopped crying. He picked up a stone, flung it with force out into the road and this made her laugh harder. I threw away my binoculars and let them slide down the slope.

I was now completely on my own, isolated, as if I'd woken from surgery to discover I was missing my legs. Or maybe my dick. I was afraid and couldn't believe I had fallen into a void like this. There was no way out. But at this point my guts broke in and I went to find food.

At the supermarket, the boss (also known as the cashier) was drinking from a large Thermos of boiling water and chewing on a roll. There were at least four or five more packets beside her. She kept eating and it reminded me of Ma. She would always sit at home alone, eating the out-of-date food she brought back from work.

'Could you stop eating for a second?'

She stopped chewing. I took out twenty *yuan*.

'Throw that shit away.'

She took the money, but was puzzled. I turned just as I was leaving. She drank another gulp of water and stuffed the remaining bread in her mouth.

I approached a noodle shop. The young girl in the doorway bowed: 'Welcome.' I looked at her tightly pressed lips. How strange, I thought. I watched as another customer arrived. Yet again, the words came out but her lips didn't move. It was a supernatural power, like those guys on the street who hand out leaflets and somehow always manage to slice them into people's hands like a knife through turnip.

The meaning of life:

Boredom.
Repetition.
Order.
Entrapment.
Imprisonment.

I spent twenty *yuan* to have a shower in the public baths and another ten to stay the night. I rested on the sofa in the main hall and, for the first time in ages, watched TV. The anchor was a woman, dressed in blue and with a slight wave in her hair. She looked proper, but her voice was hard like bullets. She fired a whole box of them. Not one mistake. She must have had years of elocution lessons. It made me feel like all the news broadcasts were somehow filtered through her brain. Everything was reported in the same tone, whether the news was happy, tragic, outrageous or mundane.

She finished telling the viewers that 'two hundred citizens have been engulfed in a forest fire', turned over her papers and continued. 'Today more than thirty people were killed when a suicide bomb exploded.' I listened as she read on, smiled and announced the end of the programme. Nothing about me. I'd been forgotten. Or replaced. I had always thought news broadcasting to be a righteous enterprise, but now I knew there was nothing more shameless. It takes victims by the hand with hot tears in its eyes, listens to them pour their heart out and drops them again as soon as something new comes along. It's all about feeding the consumers with the spiciest informational treats. I was past my sell-by date. I'd lost my notoriety. I was beginning to feel bored with myself too.

Just then I heard noises in the hall answering each other, infecting each other, like a herd of hippos grunting at each other. I kept jumping to my feet, looking for wire to tie around their fleshy necks (and strangle the crap out of them). The girl at the front desk noticed my discomfort and led me upstairs, where I could rest in peace.

She gave me a single room and an old mother figure came in, carrying a bag. I was a wreck. All because she went into the bathroom and took off her T-shirt, undid her bra and removed her trousers and underpants, as if she was at home. I could see her flabby yellow breasts, bellybutton and her pudenda. For me, sex should be mystical, like an offering to the gods. It has to start with rituals. But she was presenting her privates like a plate of melon seeds. I shrank back into the bed as she pulled my trousers down. She grabbed hold of my erection and tugged roughly (it felt like sandpaper). I begged her to stop, but she rubbed her knees and climbed up. She then prised herself apart and sat on my cock. I tried pushing her away, but she flattened me like a steamroller. She screamed as if in pain. I mumbled something, but she was immersed in her work.

'Enough!'

She fell silent, but she kept grinding.

'I'm done,' I said.

'Oh,' she said, rubbing her lower belly and picking herself up unceremoniously.

She stepped quickly into her pants. I reached out sadly, trying to get her to wait. But she dressed, put on her ugly high heels and left.

I went to the second floor, where the sound of snoring formed a chorus that was getting louder and louder and continued downwards into the baths. The attendant thrust a towel in my hands and smiled. There was meaning in that smile, I thought. The old woman had told everyone that I shot my load too early. 'That boy, he was barely in before he came!' It was humiliating.

I spent the night curled up in bed and couldn't sleep. Some screws must have come loose at the joins in the water pipes. The gurgling sound was like a crawling gecko, until a roar of water echoed around the otherwise quiet bathhouse. Like a meteorite shower splashing into the ocean. The loneliness was like a slaughter.

The next morning I got on a bus to the Western Hills. In ancient times they were known as the Qin Mountains, as China's first emperor, Qin Shihuang, was supposed to have reached this spot after conquering the Warring States, forming roads with his whip and slicing mountains with his sword. I was just here for the view from the top, where I could catch the sunrise. I wasn't the only one to have the same idea, so we sat together in the darkness, like strangers in a doctor's waiting room.

The sky slowly turned from blue to faded red. It was coming in from the sea. When the sun came peeping from behind the clouds, everyone whooped for joy, but I was disappointed. To be honest it looked a floating orange ping-pong ball gradually moving closer, hotter, spreading its arms out towards us. I was scared, as if I was being examined. I couldn't escape its evil clutches.

In its overenthusiasm, the sun spat out tongues of fire. At first it was like a ball of dry grass going up in flames, a fireball at its centre and with dry singed outer edges. I could no longer look at it straight. Eventually the metal and rays of light began to melt and fall. It was leaving us, as if trying to flee the sky. A bright black hole burning in it. Then a freeze-frame. And it was back to being that normal sun, the one we see every day. My skin was greasy and my clothes were wet. I was itchy all over. I hadn't had enough sleep and felt like being sick.

I took my bag and walked down the other side of the hill, where there was still some shade. I checked there was no one around, put down my bag and suddenly cried out, 'I'm here!'

The sound was like a stone skimmed across the water's surface, as it travelled up through each layer of cloud and out into the sky. Then I took out the last three banknotes in my possession. Their serial numbers ended with 1, 2 and 3 respectively.

1. Keep running.
2. Give myself up.
3. Suicide.

I would listen to God. I folded and mixed them until I could no longer tell them apart. I reached for one, but unfolded another. HQ24947723. A crooked name written in ballpoint pen: Li Jixi. It had once been in the possession of a poor peasant. And now it wanted me to kill myself.

I removed a nylon rope from my bag (I had planned for this) and started patting nearby trees like a carpenter. I chose one that must have been at least a hundred years old, one that had calmly faced down hail, lightning and snowstorms and would continue to do so for some time to come. I carried two stones, stacked them, knotted the rope and fastened it to a thick branch above. I looked around me. Beyond the dense forest a road circled and beyond that I could see small box-like houses with people crawling around them like insects.

I stepped up and secured the rope around my neck. I kicked away the stones and felt my body plummet, only to then get jerked back up again, as if the lift I'd be been riding had lost control. It all happened in slow motion, but before I knew it I was hanging, the rope digging into my neck. I felt the blood surge upwards, but it quickly sank back down. Then a pain and itch in my extremities, followed by numbness. The only thing I could feel was above the neck. It was as if my insides had been squeezed out of my body by a car.

The sky was receding ever higher as I swung from the branch. In the distance I could hear the sound of splitting wood. I continued to hang for a few moments and then dropped like a bag of pork to the ground. I lay there, trying to catch my breath, before ripping away at the claws around my throat. But I couldn't loosen the rope, so I scrambled to my feet and stumbled on. I wasn't dying but it had to come off. I was going crazy.

I don't remember who cut the rope, someone with a knife. But I recall my body's first reaction to freedom was to erupt in a violent fit, calmed only as the blood returned to my limbs. I stood up. The sweat poured off me and my trousers were weighed down with shit, but I pushed through the crowd of tourists and made my way down the hill. I was starving. I washed myself in the cold lake water and decided never to do that again.

Midway down the hill was a small village. Shop flags fluttered in the wind and plumes of steam from baskets of buns filled the air. Locals were laying out displays of walnuts and almonds by a line of parked buses, with tour groups poking at their wares. I'd stepped out of a cold and desolate world into one of warmth and sensuality. They knew nothing of what I'd been through, the horror that had just befallen me.

Breakfast restored me and I went to find a telephone kiosk.

'Who is this?' the voice from the other end said, clearly shaken.

'Li Yong, it's me.'

'Who?'

'Me.'

His silence told me he knew.

'Don't worry. I just called to say one thing. Remember this day and raise a glass to me every year. I'll be your brother in the next life too.'

The idiot started crying. 'Of course.'

I had planned to ask him what people were saying about me, but I decided I could well imagine. So I hung up.

I found a shady billiard shack, picked up a cue and started playing. The boss wanted the business, so he came over to play with me. I took out my last three hundred and placed them under a stone at the edge of the table. 'One hundred a game.' The boss looked me up and down and said we should play a game first.

It was just as well, as he was an impatient guy who didn't put any thought into his shots. Balls that needed only the lightest nudge, he'd thwack. I played carefully, trying to prolong the game with tactics. It wasn't my usual style, but right now I thought it might not be a bad option. It was like playing mah-jong with the boss; you had to let him win, but not too easily. He accused me at times of taking too long. He had a dirty mouth and after a while I too started recklessly smashing balls. At least that way he stayed and played.

I was controlling him and I wasn't going to let the game finish just yet. Only when a group of guys came in did I let my real skills show, leaving the boss reeling in shock.

'I just wanted you to help me kill time.'

He looked insulted, picked up the cue and started thumping it against the table. I didn't look at him but went over to the refrigerator, took out a cola and a packet of cigarettes and dropped a hundred note.

'Keep the change.'

I drank a long gulp of the cola, puffed on a cigarette and examined the suits who had just strode in. They looked over a few times, but dismissed me.

'Who you looking for?' I asked gruffly.

They came over. One took out a photo and showed it to me. I was looking at a picture of myself with a grisly beard and messy hair. I was staring down the lens. I don't think I'd have recognised myself either.

'What a bunch of novices.'

They looked insulted and turned to leave. I blew out a curl of smoke and reached out as it clouded my eyes.

'I killed Kong Jie.'

I only said it because of the smoke in my eyes.

They looked at each other and then swarmed around me, pushing at my shoulders, stamping on my legs, trying to wrestle me to the floor.

'I could have been long gone, if I'd wanted to.'

Once in the back of the car, they treated me with a

bit more reverence. I was a murderer, after all, not just some tramp. In fact, they handled me like an expensive ceramic vase, afraid I'd break. They couldn't hide their latent narcissism, though.

'How did you know who we were?'

'The leather belts.'

They looked down at their waists. The buckles were printed with a police crest.

'I want a KFC,' I said, and then dropped off to sleep.

The Interrogation

They covered my head. The sound of their voices was distant; it felt like I was the only one in the car. We drove faster and faster until suddenly we came to a stop. Firecrackers were exploding outside the window and a commanding officer barked some instructions. I was pulled out of the car and made to walk. I heard the *pa-pa-pa* of camera shutters. Everything was sharp, bumping into me, until up ahead the road emptied, where it was like being pushed towards the lonely night.

They lifted the cloth from my head and I saw walls. A metal door. A window pulled shut. They pushed a piece of paper towards me to sign and then attached me by the hands to the metal loops fastened to the wall. I couldn't stand properly, only on my tiptoes. I protested and their response was to fetter my feet. I decided not to make any more requests.

My body kept sinking and I had to fight for the right to rest. Sometimes my poor hands would let my feet take the burden, sometimes the other way round.

'I need a pee!' I shouted at one point, the response to which was the sound of clanging from outside and then, 'Go on then.'

The urine ran down my trousers and thighs and out between my toes, like a bottle of warm, spilt milk. There must have been a camera. I was being watched. I figured I might as well fart a few times, spit on the wall, talk to myself. I wasn't going to get to sleep. I was starting to feel jealous of people who were free to hang themselves from bridges, or get beaten up.

As the light disappeared, they came to undo my handcuffs. I flopped to the ground. They dragged me into a dark room, placed me on a low chair and then disappeared. Just as I drifted into sleep a terrifying light shone in my face. It looked like one of those lights photographers use that burn your skin. I squinted. A fluorescent lamp above followed, its dim light falling like a waterfall onto a head of dense silver hair before me. I could only make out an outline of the man, sitting proudly. He was chewing. I could hear the sound of his tongue slurping as he licked his fingers.

'You should always eat chicken wings while they're still hot, or the fat coagulates as they cool and they lose their taste.'

I wasn't unsympathetic to this opinion.

I felt the heat pulsing through my brain like an electrical current, but I wasn't sweaty. I just wished I was dead, to be honest. I tried to ask a few times when we could start, but it was no good. That was like a woman asking a thug, 'When are you going to start raping me?'

He ate twelve chicken wings in all (he was definitely going to have a case of the runs when he got home). Then, finally, he spoke.

'Name.'

Then the questions came ringing out one after another.

Date and place of birth.

Address.

Qualifications.

'Date of birth,' he repeated.

I told him again.

'Are you sure?'

'Yes.'

I realised that he was checking to be sure I had turned eighteen. He picked his teeth with a toothpick. I was about to collapse when he broke the silence again.

'You must know that resistance is futile.'

'I know.'

'So you know why we were looking for you?'

I'd never heard such a stupid question. They'd called on the general public, arranged planning meetings, brought in experienced cops, investigated my background with the help of psychologists. And, of course, they designed their interrogation. This was the way to do it, apparently. Little did they know, all they had to do was ask.

'I killed Kong Jie,' I fired back. 'I killed her ruthlessly, stabbed her over and over until her blood ran like a river.'

'Write it down.'

Only then did I realise there was another policeman in the corner. I could tell from the rustle of his pen that they were excited beyond their wildest dreams. I was desperate to sleep, so I answered their questions quickly, including how I'd convinced her to come over, how I killed her, what I did with the body and how I ran away. I was like a rich landlord handing out charity parcels to his poor tenants.

Then I said, 'Water.'

'Why did you kill her?'

'Water.'

'We'll give you water after you answer.'

This was a stinking deal, it struck me. I still had my dignity after all.

'Please continue,' they said.

But I turned my head and waited, without looking at them. They took the lid off the jar and were about to water me, when I raised my head up high.

'We can convict you with the evidence, we don't need your confession,' the old guy said.

'Then get to it.'

He tapped his pen awkwardly and waved his hands.

The other policeman gave me his notes.

'No need,' I said, and signed it.

He told me I still had to read it, but I just wrote: *I hereby declare that I have read and confirm there are no mistakes.*

Not long after, they took me back to the military academy apartments. The police had cordoned off the area, but that hadn't stopped a crowd gathering. Wherever I went, they swarmed after me. I was an animal in a zoo. I looked out at them and smiled. This provoked a middle-aged man, who moved through the crowd holding up a stick as if to hit me, to beat me with the morality I had been missing all along. I struggled, wanting to hit him back. The others retreated. Only he stood firm.

The trees had turned yellow.

In the past, I never took any notice of the cycle of leaves growing and wilting. But now they were yellow. The last time I would see them turn yellow. My neighbour, Mr He, led the way, resolute but silent. I could almost see the dust rising beneath his feet. In the event of corners or stairs, he would extend his right hand as a signal to the rear. Once his duties as public security activist were completed, he hung around watching, following. As if they might consult him at any time for his expert opinion. But there was no need to trouble him with such matters.

I went to the door of Auntie's apartment and looked out at the sky. It was empty, peaceful in its deepest reaches. A death omen, I said to myself.

The windows on both sides of my old room were sealed shut and the washing machine had been placed by the door. The tape had been removed and stuck to the wall. They pulled the light switch, gave me a plastic doll and knife and asked me to begin. But I didn't know how.

'Kill her,' they said.

My uniform didn't have pockets, so I stuck the knife into my waistband. I held the model from behind, covered her nose and mouth. I stood still.

'Keep going,' they said.

'She fought back.'

'Move her yourself.'

I swayed her in my arms, whispered in her ear, let go and pulled out the tape. I covered her mouth and then tore it away. I started screaming.

They shrank back at first, then surrounded me.

'That's her screaming,' I said.

'That bit you can leave out.'

'No, I can't.'

I started screaming again, quite the actor. I covered

her mouth, took the knife from my waist and jabbed it at her abdomen. Unfortunately the blade just slid, rather than piercing. But I kept stabbing her. I pushed her over to the window and drew back the curtain with the knife. I let go of the model again and began retching against the wall. I then crouched, scratched her face and held her down.

At that moment everything felt blurry (like when the washerwoman stops what she's doing and stares into space). A large shadow on the wall. Crazed blows, as if I was really stabbing her. They were replaying everything, the shadows, and I felt a twitching in the darkest recesses of my memory.

I took her into my arms, tipped her updside down into the washing machine and said, 'It was a switchblade, I seem to remember.'

I thought they might ask me to show them some other locations in this pongy city, but they said there was no need. The policeman who'd fallen from the motorbike was lucky, he was doing fine now.

The next day we moved to a meeting room, which consisted of a red table reflecting the afternoon light. A female officer brewed some tea for me while the others set up a camera and opened their notebooks. They took their seats opposite. As if we were all sitting down to a plain old meeting. The old man's face was like stone, his skin lumpy and his features sunken (especially his nose, which was nothing more than two nostrils). Maybe he'd had leprosy. He was hideous; his cold eyes were pulverising my insides. Just like the first time, I'd tell them everything calmly.

I looked down, the tea cup gripped in my hands, and examined the links between the handcuffs.

'Head up.'

I looked up.

'Look at me.'

The old man was forcing me to look him in the eyes and it felt like I was disappearing. I was a pile of burning firewood, my body crackled, the cup shook and the boiling water splashed out and scalded me.

It's hard for me to describe what happened that day. You probably won't believe me. I felt like I was walking into a tunnel, while the old man retreated, beckoning me towards the light at the other end. I followed in silence, I had no choice. If he asked the same questions as the last time, I would tell him everything. But he only prompted me to go through the incident again. So I started from the beginning. The texts, the whispers, the struggles, the tape, the switchblade, the curtain, the washing machine. He kept nodding, while the man next to him solemnly made notes, his eyes soft and encouraging. But I was fed up. I hate having to repeat things.

'Then what?' he said.

'Nothing,' I said.

I'd done my duty, so I leaned down on the table to sleep. One of the officers grabbed my head and I wrestled free. The old man kept gesturing for me to continue.

'Let's talk about why. You say you put her upside down in the washing machine. Why did you do that?'

'No reason.'

'OK, then when you let go of her in front of the window, was she already dead?'

'Must have been.'

'Are you sure?'

'I can't be sure, but I think she must have been.'

'So if she was already dead, why did you stab her thirty-seven times?'

'No reason.'

'You know what? Our old medical expert has never vomited at a crime scene. But after seeing what happened to that girl she was such a nervous wreck she went into hospital. The girl lost enough blood to fill the washing machine half full. The medical examiner said she'd never seen anything like it – the murderer must have been completely consumed with hatred.' He rubbed his eyes. 'Why did you hate her so much?'

'I didn't hate her.'

'That doesn't seem possible.'

'Really.'

'If that's the case, why do something so brutal, so ruthless?'

'No reason.'

He threw his tea cup to the floor, making his colleague jump. He leaned forward and banged on the table. 'No reason?' he roared.

I looked down and said nothing. The direction he was taking and his methods were all wrong. He was making a big mistake.

'Speak,' he said, thumping the table.

'I have nothing to say.'

He walked over, grabbed my collar and raised a clenched fist. But I wasn't scared. If he hit me on the left cheek, I'd give him my right as well. Winners don't get so easily flustered. His colleague kept telling him to stop, but it took some time for him to calm down. Then he started telling me about his son who was about my age. His tone changed, as if talking to a friend. After having flunked his college entrance exams his son ran away. When the old man found him, he beat him. But beating his son was like beating himself.

'After that I realised there was nothing I could not forgive. There is nothing in life too big that it cannot be forgiven.'

He was in a world of his own emotions and, with tears in his eyes, he looked at me.

'We'll get through this crisis together. Kid, was there really no other way to solve your problems with Kong Jie?'

'We didn't have any.'

'And yet you stabbed her another thirty-seven times, after she was already dead?'

'You don't get it.'

'You liked her but she didn't feel the same way, is that it?'

'No.'

'Did she humiliate you?'

'No.'

'Then why?'

I looked straight at him. 'I'd like to know the answer to that too.'

Blood pumped into his cheeks and he looked as sombre as a stick of dynamite. He walked over to the TV screen, trembling, and picked up a photo frame. His hands wouldn't stop shaking.

'Who is he?' he said in a stutter.

'My father.'

Pa looked exhausted, his skin barely stretched over his skeleton. He was in the last stages of his cancer, but still he managed to smile at the camera. I thought about his birth, his childhood, where he went to school, his work at the mine and finally marriage, a kid, sickness and death. To put it bluntly, he was born and then he died. Just like everyone else. Just like the old investigator who was getting nowhere. Just like the kid sitting in front of him.

'Do you know who provided for you, brought you up?' he said, waving the frame.

I didn't answer.

'Do you know what he went through?' He answered himself: 'Cancer.' He then started on the poor-parents-and-all-they-go-through routine. 'Don't you feel sorry for what you've done to him?'

'Immensely.'

He turned to the others.

'Am I right? We all have parents who have sacrificed themselves?'

At first they were stunned, looked at each other and murmured their agreement. It was a vulgar game. He placed the picture of my father in front of me, hoping for remorse.

'How about telling him, from your heart?'

'Nope.'

The other policemen were at least amused with my reply.

I smiled and repeated, 'I'm not going to do that.'

The inspector stood up, overturning his chair, and blew like a steam engine.

'You animal! You animal! Get out of my sight!' he roared with a wave of his hand.

And with that the interrogation was over.

The Game

The mystery of why I had killed Kong Jie attracted much attention among the general public. Speculation provided an opportunity for people to prove themselves more intelligent than their peers. Discussions were animated. Nothing was taken for granted: some read my letters and the notes scribbled in my textbooks; others interviewed my classmates, teachers and relatives. But I united them all in feelings of frustration when it came to the question of motive. I was holding the cards, after all, so why not play for a bit?

It also made the other inmates jealous.

Guys in prison are usually society's weirdos and with that reputation comes their own private sense of dignity. They don't talk about their crimes, like the stupid stuff you do when drunk. But different crimes demand different levels of respect. The murderers, for example, were consistently more arrogant than the petty thieves. They asked me what I was in for, but once I told them I'd killed a girl, stabbed her thirty-seven times leaving her innards spilling out and head down in a washing machine, they never spoke to me again.

Every time I was called out for questioning, they

whistled in anger. 'Off for another spanking!' It was all to do with saving face. Their crimes had been explained away long ago.

One night I crept into a corner, a ghost, while the others snored under their blankets. But just as I was about to take a piss they surrounded me, putting me in a headlock. I'd heard of this before. I jumped and screamed.

They were suffocating me.

I don't know how many times they punched and slapped me, like a farmer beating the ground with his threshing paddle. They then emptied the communal bucket of piss over my head. It didn't feel like liquid, but more like solid fat. It knocked my head to one side. One of the prison officers grabbed me by the hair and nearly twisted my neck off.

'Making a scene, huh?' he said.

'Why did you kill her?' he continued.

I refused to give an answer. Just as his fist was about to smash into my cheek, I caught a whiff of its meaty smell. My body shook and I began howling.

'My aunt! Because of my aunt!'

'Your aunt?'

'My aunt abused me.'

'What's that got to do with the girl?'

'I wanted her to know I'm not a pushover.'

His voice was raspy, fierce and uncontrolled, as if his vocal cords had been scraped against an iron file. Everyone else started laughing, their voices like flowers in a country meadow. My answer may have been amusing, but at least it satisfied them.

'You could've killed your aunt. Why the girl?' the prison officer said.

'My aunt's strong. It was easier to kill the girl.'

The officer gestured to the others not to laugh.

'And to think I thought you might have been someone.'

The others bent over, gasping, 'strong', 'easier', jumping around in their laughter. This lasted for some time. I decided to take a lesson from my favourite Hong Kong films. It was all a matter of patience. I could spend years grinding down my toothbrush, until it was sharp enough to murder them. Then I'd take them, one by one.

I looked at the overturned piss pot lying on the floor and tears of humiliation ran down my cheeks. The officer was yawning and flapped the blanket over his flabby belly. I tossed the wet towel on the floor, picked up the piss bucket and smashed it down on his head. He fell to the ground. Then I started smashing his face as if it was a stone. I nearly pulverised him.

Thinking he was dead, I turned to my fellow inmates, now trembling. But at that moment, the officer grabbed hold of my trouser leg. I heard him spit blood, then he spoke.

'Go on, kill me.'

I picked up the bucket and hit him again. He gasped, his limbs twitched out and he fell unconscious.

'He asked me to kill him,' I said to the others, quietly. But it sounded too soft. 'I've already murdered one person. Doesn't make much difference now,' I snarled.

The inmates seemed to realise that something was up and started beating at their washbasins. The officers came rushing and tried to bring order, but the cells were rowdy, like the boys' changing room after PE.

I was put into solitary.

Again, the investigator asked me, 'Why did you kill Kong Jie?'

'Because I hate my aunt.'

'But why kill Kong Jie if the person you hate is your aunt?'

'I couldn't kill my aunt, but I wanted her to know I'm not a pushover.'

It was a forced kind of logic, I know, but it was good enough. In order to make it more persuasive, I added something about wanting to rape Kong Jie, and then I decided to implicate old Mr He next door by making up something about how he and my aunt had hurt me badly. That they were in cahoots. I finished with some bull about my aunt being a country woman with the mindset of a petty capitalist. This made their eyes light up. The loose links of my logic had now become tight and unbreakable, all because of these buzzwords. I was feeling pretty satisfied.

In truth, it's pretty difficult to kill a man. On one of our breaks outside, I saw the officer being led around, his face blue and swollen. He spotted me and in his eyes I saw panic because he couldn't get his revenge. He wasn't faking it. If it hadn't been for the other guards, he would have accepted the death penalty as a price worth paying for being able to run over to me there and then and strangle me. I looked at him out of the corner of my eye, almost coquettishly. This would probably make him more sick.

A few days later I was led into a meeting room. I sat waiting until the door opened and then a man wearing reading glasses and with neatly combed white hair walked in. He bowed to each of the prosecutors, one by one.

'Excellent, excellent,' he said.

My first impressions were not good. This guy was a running dog if ever I'd seen one.

He acted like we were old acquaintances, asking me politely where he should sit. Wherever, I said. He said he didn't want to cause me any pressure. Finally he moved a bench over and sat in front of me. Only then did I realise that he was right, having him sit in front of me like this made me feel trapped in his gaze. It was pretty uncomfortable. But I didn't say anything.

'Relax,' he said. 'I'm not a policeman and I don't work for the judiciary. I have no legal right to punish or incarcerate you and I'm not here to pass judgement. I'm an old man of sixty-four and you are only nineteen, but here we are equals. I want us to talk, open up. Fate has brought us together.'

I took his business card:

Vice-President of the City Education Association
Member of the Provincial Family Education Research Unit

He watched me read it, then said, 'I'm just an ordinary citizen.'

He took out a packet of cigarettes and asked if I wanted one. I accepted without saying anything and he leaned over to light it. I remembered a film I saw once where a man lit a cigarette like this and was then captured by the prisoner and taken hostage himself. The lighter wouldn't produce a flame, but he kept flicking patiently. I was starting to like him. Maybe I could tell him some personal things. The thought was a beautiful one, in the same way mathematics is beautiful and in that beauty you can find comfort. I needed the right person to listen. I just wanted him to listen.

He took a pile of loose papers from his briefcase, licked his finger and began flicking through them. They were covered in red notes. He put some to one side. He carried on like this for some time. I smoked alone. It was my first cigarette in ages and I was surprised by the taste. It almost tasted of shit. I felt dizzy, like I'd been drinking cheap booze. The sun came flooding through the window. I'd been longing for it while alone in my cell, but now I just felt hot and itchy.

Eventually he finished tidying the papers on the table, looked up. 'Uh huh.' He pinched the fingers of his left hand together (as if catching a mosquito) and spoke.

'Do you think this kind of incident is an exception or quite common in today's society?'

'An exception.'

'Uh huh. It does seem to be an exception, but in fact exceptionality and normality are united in their opposition. Normal behaviour contains abnormal behaviour and exceptional incidents embody society's norms. We must find the reason here.'

The chances of us talking had been ruined. He was

right, but it was the kind of right that gave no moral nourishment. I had no idea what he was doing here, other than showing off his education. He was like an old sheep, soft and warm, kind-looking. He could have decided to be a good listener.

Suddenly he asked me who I lived with before the age of five.

'Grandpa and Grandma.'

'What did they give you?'

'Love.'

'What kind of love?'

'Unconditional. They spoilt me.'

'To what degree?'

I began talking, it flowed out, moving stories of their love. His pen moved quickly. In the gaps between my stories he drew lines in his papers, as if solving a mathematical problem. He wanted answers and that made me despise him. If he'd given the matter two seconds' thought, he would have realised no one could have such clear memories of life before they turned five. I reminisced about my short life just as he requested: when I went back to live with my parents, when I left again, my moves between schools in the village, county town and provincial capital, the pressures and troubles that had brought me to my critical juncture.

'Do you think leaving the life in which you were the

object of your grandparents' love was beneficial or detrimental to you?'

'It did much more harm than good. It's essentially the reason I killed Kong Jie.'

He was jumping with excitement, as was his pen on the page. He made one last stab in his notes. Full stop. He took to his feet like a scientist who had discovered a new wonder cure or a writer who had just finished his masterwork. Caught in the ecstasy of creation. He would probably have embraced me had it not been for the armed police in the room. Controlling himself, he feigned a pained expression.

'You, son, are a typical case of a fallen prince.'

'No, I'm the redeemer.'

I brushed him away, my heart filled with loathing and bitter disappointment.

Two days later I was led once again into the meeting room with the same camera set up. I felt an overwhelming weight, like I was standing high up on a stage, my lapels fluttering in the wind, and thousands of expectant faces looking up at me. I was used to straightening my hunched spine, putting on a show of spiritedness, but not capriciousness. It was a painstaking performance, a completely different me.

The person sitting before me, trying to make me feel

comfortable, was a female journalist. The table had been removed, there was nothing between us. She had short, permed hair, alabaster skin and an ever so slightly plump, round face. She wore a hemp-grey Western suit jacket and navy skirt. She was leaning forward, her fingers criss-crossed and placed on her raised knees, smiling (as if smiling was the mouth's only function). Her chin was raised, ever so slightly looking up. Her eyes never left me.

It was like being cursed. I felt a sudden urge to plead with her. I was awaiting her instructions.

'Don't think about the camera,' she said.

'Uh huh.'

I was shy. Her teeth were white and straight, the tone of her voice warm, like a breeze flitting through leaves, deep and richly magnetic. Every word was itself a form of clarity.

She passed me the morning paper. The vice-president of the City Education Association had concluded that there were three contributing factors as to why I had committed murder:

1. A failure in my upbringing.
2. Pressure resulting from the college entrance exams.
3. Negative societal influence.

He finished with more nonsense, meant to prevent

similar incidents in the future:

1. Understanding and comprehension.
2. Attention and patience.
3. Equality and reciprocity.

'What do you think?' she asked me.

'Bullshit.'

I already knew what she wanted. She smiled broadly.

'Then why do you think you did it?'

'Diversion. I'd say diversion.'

'What did you want diversion from?'

She nodded, her eyes leading me on. I was desperate to speak. I began telling her the truth, one sentence, two sentences, but then in burst a middle-aged man (like a lion trespassing into our territory, she was my lioness). He was clutching a piece of paper which she read, reclined in her seat and exchanged meaningful looks with him as he left.

That was it, it was over, whatever there had been between us. I shut my mouth.

'Diversion from what?' she asked with a heavy heart, having seemingly forgotten my earlier explanation.

'Nothing,' I said.

Then I said, 'For a moment, you reminded me of my cousin.'

She liked this and leaned forward again. It was the

most hypocritical thing I'd ever witnessed. To think I'd thought her worth trusting, just like my cousin. Now I could see that supposed sincerity for what it was, a superficial technique. She was trying to cheat an answer out of me. Everything was leading to this; even her dress and make-up were carefully chosen to this end. As soon as I'd given her what she wanted, she would leave, high-fiving her colleagues on a job well done.

'Please continue with what you were saying,' she said.

'I've got nothing to say,' I said.

The atmosphere became frosty and she wasn't expecting it. In one last-ditch attempt, she started an onslaught of ridiculous questions.

'What does it feel like to be sent away from home?'

'It's not what you're thinking, I wasn't constantly burning with anger.'

This was possibly my last offer of kindness, but she didn't take it. Instead she rushed to the next question.

'What was it that stopped you from putting the fire out?'

'Putting the fire out?'

'I mean, the flames of your rage, your desire to kill?'

'It was impossible.'

'How come?'

'Because the ground beneath me was burning.'

'So you just let the flames grow?'

'I didn't let them grow, they were going to grow without me.'

We carried on like this, not fully understanding each other, until she decided she had had enough. She turned her back on me and spoke to the camera. She read the words beautifully:

Resplendent flowering youth, joy and wild abandon
suddenly, this was the outcome
My heart, what pain?
Child, I don't understand
Why would you do such a thing?
I hear mother's blood-filled tears
Child, I lament
I cannot, will never comprehend
why you would do such a thing.

I wanted to cry. If I'd known someone was going to write such a shit poem, I wouldn't have killed her.

In Prison

No one came to visit after that. I was handcuffed and tied by my feet, like a bear in captivity. After hours of sitting for too long, I began to feel like I'd become stuck to the cold, damp floor, that I had become part of the building. I'd heard people say that prisoners could spend a whole afternoon playing with one ant and eventually were able to distinguish between males and females. But there were no insects here, so I had my hands on my crotch most of the time. In, out. My hands were sticky from semen and smelt like a fish market. I took to wiping them on the soles of my feet until they were black with grime. I didn't do it for pleasure, I was just bored senseless.

I asked the guard for a Rubik's cube, but was refused. I said it wasn't exactly a lot to ask.

'What would be the point of locking you up if I were to give you a Rubik's cube?'

He pulled the small metal window shut and I start thumping at it.

'What's a Rubik's cube got to do with my incarceration?'

He ignored me. I asked him again when he came with food.

'You want to play with the Rubik's cube. If I gave you one, I would be undermining any sense of punishment.' He was kind of right.

I started obsessing over my arrest; the blue skies of freedom outside my window didn't occupy my thoughts much. I could have pushed over the police officer and run. I could have used stones or a kitchen knife to keep passers-by away. They would probably have shot me. Instead, I sat alone in my cell facing the immeasurable void that was time itself. Life's petty problems (frustrated commutes, tedious work, inconsequential arguments, sexual escapades) were all designed to create a screen between the flesh and time's inevitable stranglehold. But I was stuck in my cell, with nothing to do, or at least nothing that could keep me occupied for more than a few minutes, and time's infinite embrace kept leaning towards me. Herculean, invincible, omniscient, flesh without feeling, it listened not to your entreaties, cared not for your sorrows, it was the dirt always crushed, the waves always crashing, it forced itself into every space, drowned you, dismembered you, it pressed on top of you so that its weight felt solid, it dug into you like a quick, relentless bamboo arrow piercing through your nails. There was no resisting it. It was a slow demise. My father's image came to me and hot tears gathered in my eyes.

In the days before my father's death, he stayed in a hospital room much like my cell – cramped, dark and moist, the floor like rat skin giving off the stench of nothingness. At one point, having been in a coma for a while, he quietly woke and took my hand.

'I keep seeing a young man in a white robe sitting over there by the wall. I think I know him, but at the same time I don't. He is eating a simple apple. Or maybe he is simply eating an apple. Can you hear the chewing? He sits with his back pressed against the wall, his eyes shut, concentrating on the piece of fruit. He will never finish. He is waiting for the right moment to stand up. He will throw the pips on the floor, step on them. He is waiting, but you don't know what for.

'He is the angel of death,' he continued. 'He has come to tell you that death is not a flash or an exclamation mark. It doesn't come suddenly, in a violent moment. It is a process. Your organs are waiting to malfunction, one by one, like a water bottle cooling. It's not about waiting for that one painful moment. Child, what I really want is for someone to lie down beside me and die with me. But that rarely happens in life. I see only you healthy people, growing. You frown, you cry, but you still have energy in your bones. Your bodies are like buds after the spring rains. I was exhausted long ago. You come only to reinforce this truth. You've locked me in this cell, but you are outside running like children in a playground. Your laughter is like a metal weight pressing on me, pinning me down. I feel ashamed of you. There is such a distance between us. Either fuck off, or get a gun and shoot me.'

My father sighed, his dreadful attempt at a poetic monologue over, and finally brushed me away in disgust. I left, thinking of the injustice of it all. You're born, you get old, you get sick, you die. Oh, humanity! It's nothing but a fucking disgrace. All of it. But as soon as my mother walked in, my father rolled into her arms and cried. Ma didn't say anything to comfort him.

I started trying to keep up with life outside my cell. I would scrape my finger along the dusty floor and mark the days on the wall. But I soon gave up. I was going to die whatever, so what was the point? Time turned into a primal chaos, days could pass in what felt like only one, or they went on for ever (like broken shards of glass, impossible to count). Sometimes I wanted to keep the night from coming and other days I longed for it to come quickly, even when it might already have been dark outside. My dreams became more vivid. Once I pictured myself in bed. I went to get up, to visit someone, but I was paralysed. This was the only person in the whole world whom I cared about and who felt the same way about me. There were no feelings of resentment between us. I couldn't see his face, he had no name. I went through everyone I had ever met, but there was no such person. But when he brushed against the clouds, the branches and the occasional lightning when he flew up into the sky, at that moment I felt I knew him better than I would ever know another human being. He shook his scales and from them drops of water rained.

'I dreamed of you, so I came,' he said.

'Who are you?'

'I am the person in your dreams.'

'Then who am I?'

'You are the person in my dreams.'

'Do you exist here on Earth?'

'No.'

'What about me?'

'Neither do you.'

'But I felt it, when you pinched my hand.'

'We don't exist.'

'I want to die.'

'I dreamed that you died. But I can also dream that you live.'

'Then dream that I live.'

'It doesn't make a difference.'

I woke up and felt amused. I started imagining I was

a character in a novel. I saw a hunched author sitting in the glow of a lamp. He wrote my name on a white piece of paper before adding more detail: my clothes, where I lived, my school and friends, general personality traits, my life story, what would happen to me. And I in turn outlined his life. Every time my mind speeded up, I instructed myself to slow down. I planned it all, down to the songs he listened to when writing. He chose ten or so from his collection and listened to each in turn until the sounds of 'Silver Springs' came from his speakers. This was when he found his writing rhythm. He wrote a few sentences, but it wasn't quite flowing, so he read out loud. Anything just a little off, he excised like a ruthless despot. He stopped only when he felt it was too cruel.

'That's enough. You have to learn to forgive yourself.'

This gave him courage to continue. The inspiration had finally come, but just as he was about to throw himself into the flames of creativity, his telephone rang. A friend. He made some excuses to push the friend away, but more and more accusations came down the line. Flustered, and more than a little hostile, he sighed and went to meet the friend. He feigned interest well into the night, until the moment arrived when he could finally make his escape. But the inspiration had bolted, leaving him naked. He sat for hours, trying to catch it and bring it back, just one small bit of it, but nothing. He put his head in his hands and tried to cry, his regret as deep as the sea. He spoke to me, on the paper.

'Work sucks my energy and destroys my intellect. But I had it, just then, for a moment. Then my friends stole it from me. Why can't you give me one clean day? Why?'

'You've already given half your life to me. Why are you so desperate to kill me off?' I said to him.

'Death is the only way you'll live a little longer.'

'In that case, I'll kill you. I've murdered before.'

'No. Even if you kill me, I won't be a sell-out.'

He sucked in his cheeks and let out a long breath through his nostrils. I'd never seen anything so hilarious in my life. I patted him on the head and flew away.

I spent a lot of time absorbed in this wrestling match. Sometimes I gave form to a man in another dimension; he's been asleep for years. He made us. I tried using sex as a way of denying the reproductive order he created, but then I realised sex comes from dreams. Humans have sex, he said, and so it was. Sometimes I saw a world in my head in which humans had already been exterminated and a complex modern society was revealed to be nothing more than a mirage, a reflection in a mirror, created by a Song or Ming dynasty witch. Sometimes I scaled it down. I became merely one of ten thousand different mes. I saw them everywhere, at the docks, living apathetic lives as carpenters, or taking flights to São Paulo, or waiting in crowds for the executioner to arrive. There were times when I pictured my future grandson taking me up in his helicopter away from Shawshank Prison; if he doesn't take me away, he tells me, he won't exist in the future. He is lost in thinking, high up in his plane, until we reach our highest altitude, when he speaks.

'Actually, I only need your sperm.'

I lay like that day and night, living inside my own intricate drawings, excited to the point where I'd forget to eat and drink. If someone had come by and told me I could go free, perhaps I might have been angry to be disturbed. Where else could I find such peace? A life with no obligation to work, with free food and drink? This was the best place for me to reflect on humanity and the universe. Then, after nights of sleeplessness, my head would pound and I'd start to cry. I began to regret not considering the possibility of incarceration before committing my crime. I would have devoted myself to others, lived a healthy and harmless life. But in some ways this smugness was a product of knowing that I was soon to die – that I was locked up with nowhere to go.

The guard eventually took pity on me and gave me a piece of newspaper. He was originally going to give me one full side, but after a brief moment of reflection he took it back and ripped off a piece the size of my palm. I could have that instead. He laughed and left happy. But it was big enough. In it, I read a brilliant story with the headline: TOGETHER MAY WE EXPLODE.

One day, Tom lit a match to find out if there was any petrol left in the tank. Yep.

It kept spinning in my head and I began to invent a family saga about Tom's ancient ape-man relatives. I thanked the guard. He'd given me a perpetually bubbling spring of the sweetest water.

On Trial

I have on occasion asked myself, who is going to miss me? And I suppose my mother is the only possible answer. I thought she would visit me in prison, but after waiting for an eternity I figured she must have remarried, moved and forgotten me. Then one day one of the guards came to tell me she was here. I said I didn't want to see her, but he told me it would be good to get some fresh air and I was dragged over.

The visiting room had a high, vaulted ceiling and visitors and inmates were separated by a long, thick piece of glass. A large door at the opposite end was opened and a slow surge of free people pressed in, like a glacier, their arms outspread. Ma staggered dumbly behind, hands on the back of her thighs, her head bobbing, as if to say, 'No, no, don't hit me.' I didn't really want to see her.

She spotted me and sat down, placing a plastic bag containing a half-eaten bun in her lap. She lowered her head and said nothing, as if she was the criminal, not me. I snorted, a sneer. It was like a railway station waiting room, the noise bubbling, popping, drifting up, turning into a collective hum. Ma almost spoke several times.

'Go on, say something.'

Trembling violently, she looked up.

'Aren't you going to say what you're doing here?'

She lay out her palms, tilted her head and showed me her tears. Calluses, hard and dirty like a stone covered in weeds.

'I've been burning incense and praying.'

'What for?'

She didn't answer, but wiped her eyes with her hand.

'That's unhygienic,' I said.

She pulled at her scarf and that's when I saw how white her hair had become. Last time I saw her, she had barely one grey hair.

'What happened?'

'I woke up one morning and it was like this.'

This was the most intimate moment we'd ever shared. I tried to push my fingers through the small holes of our conversation, but I couldn't.

'Take care of yourself, Ma. Find a husband. Make sure you eat properly.'

She just shook her head. The guard approached and suddenly she seemed to realise something.

'Do what they say. And tell them everything.'

She was then led away. Or rather, she led them away. She was gone, along with her half-eaten bun. Just like that. She's no real mother.

Only when the courts sent along a copy of the indictment did I realise I'd been locked up for four months.

'We will assign you a lawyer if you don't appoint one yourself,' they said.

'What if I don't want one?'

'Most people want one.'

'OK,' I said.

They asked me if I had any evidence or witnesses I wished to present. I said no. Before long the lawyer came and asked the same question. He kept taking calls during our meeting and didn't stay long.

When the day of the trial arrived they unshackled me and led me to another cell. My feet felt light, as if I might fly up into the air. A big sign with black characters hung above the metal door, which had a window cut into it. The walls were made from greyish-white bricks. A clump of poplars grew in the yard outside, next to which an armed officer carrying an assault rifle paced, guarding his post. I looked out on the scene, the flood of morning light, the sky blue like a smashed vase. This must have been its most beautiful moment.

Ma was hiding behind the trees in the distance; I could see her peek out occasionally. As the car drove past I shouted, 'Ma! Ma!' She couldn't hear me. But I saw her frightened expression. It was in her eyes; it oppressed her. It was like watching your limbs being drawn and quartered.

At the court two policemen led me into a small room and told me to sit. I swallowed. The courtroom must have been next door, because I heard the sound of footsteps come and go. Then someone started reading the court rules and asked the public prosecutor, defence counsel, presiding judge and judicial officers to take their seats.

The judge knocked his gavel. 'Bring in the defendant.'

The metal door was pulled open and an officer took me by the arm. As if on a gust of wind, I was announced. My spirit gave way. I stood and shook my handcuffs to show my displeasure. My lawyer asked for the handcuffs to be removed, but the prosecutor objected vociferously, arguing I was a danger to the court.

Fewer than ten people were seated in the public gallery, curious spectators for the most part. One woman looked at me with poison in her eyes. She wore a black dress and a discreetly patterned scarf draped over her shoulders. She had tied a black ribbon around her arm. She looked like a lanky crow. Her skin hung loose around her face like drying noodles, the ravages of age. She pursed her lips and her nostrils flared, like a kettle ready to pop its lid. I wondered how such an ugly woman could have given birth to Kong Jie, but as Qian Zhongshu once wrote: 'Just because you liked the egg doesn't mean it is wise to go looking for the chicken.'

Before the hearing could begin the judge asked a series of meaningless questions, like my name, date of birth, ethnicity, previous criminal record, the date I had received the indictment. Finally he announced that it would be a closed trial, to respect the victim's privacy. She's dead, I thought, what privacy? He then read out a list of names and, when called, each person stood up, nodded or mmed. He then read my rights and asked if anyone should be removed from the court.

'Yes, everyone,' I said.

'Your reason?'

But I couldn't think of anything. 'Fine, let them stay.'

The public prosecutor then read aloud the indictment, as procedure dictated. He emphasised certain key words for effect, adding spices to his pot. But all things considered, he worked in an orderly fashion. Then Kong Jie's mother read out a civil indictment. Her hands shook and she made many mistakes. She wanted me to pay three hundred and twenty thousand *yuan* in damages.

Asking for money seemed a bit hypocritical, like she was trying to make money out of her daughter's death. It muddied her calls for justice. She seemed aware of it too, and so added, 'I want to make you bankrupt, that's all. I won't keep a cent of it. I'll give it all away.'

Make me bankrupt?

The judge asked for my response.

'I have to respond?'

'What is your reaction to the indictments?'

'No reaction. It's all true.'

My lawyer tapped at his table as if to ask why I wasn't defending myself, but he didn't say anything. The judge then signalled to the prosecutor to begin.

He began by confirming some more basic facts. Then, 'I have no more questions, it all seems very clear.'

The judge looked over and by mistake caught the eye of Kong Jie's mother, who took it as permission to stand up.

'Why did you kill my daughter?'

I kept my head high and said nothing.

She was shaking, her voice loud like a gale blowing over a sheet of metal. Then she groaned and sat back down. An awkward silence filled the court and those in uniform whispered to each other.

Someone needed to break the silence, so I raised my hand. The lawyer finally remembered he was on my side and signalled to the judge, who let me speak.

'Can I sit?'

My question disturbed the viewing gallery, as if this

was my primary sin. The judge thumped his gavel, but didn't answer. I wasn't sure if that was a yes, but then I thought, they're going to kill me anyway, so I plonked by butt back down on the seat. But no one cared, because the prosecutor was busy calling in the medical examiner. She was old and dressed in a white coat, her features like dead tree roots. She should have read clinically from her appraisal, giving details about how many stab wounds Kong Jie had suffered, that she died of acute blood loss trauma and so on. But the tears pumped and she kept tainting her account with 'the child' this, 'the child' that. Everything was covered in blood, the floor, the walls, the door, the window. It was horrifying. Especially the bit where I put her in the washing machine. 'Head first. The blood filled it half full.' Kong Jie's mother had been listening, wiping tears and nodding. At this point I watched her faint.

The morning's proceedings finished there. In the afternoon people tried to stop Kong Jie's mother from entering the courtroom, but she forced her way in and back to her seat. She sat watching me, hate radiating from her eyes. Suddenly, she spat at me. I spat back.

The first witness called in the afternoon was the policeman responsible for the case.

'When did you arrive at the scene?'

'The morning after.'

Kong Jie's mother stood up and pointed. 'When did you get the call?'

'I'm not sure.'

'Well, I am. I reported her missing the evening before.'

The gavel echoed around the court, but she merely spoke louder.

'I must tell the court. I rang at 6.00 the same evening, but they told me to wait twenty-four hours before reporting her missing. "Ninety-nine per cent of cases are resolved by the following morning," they said. I told them, "my daughter is a good girl, she would never run away." "Are you done?" they said. "Do you know how many cases we have to handle every day? Do you know how many officers we have? You're wasting our time." Isn't that what you said? You then said, "It's not that we don't want to take the call, but this is the law. We do as the law dictates."'

She blew her nose with her fingers, wiped it on her sleeve and continued.

'I want to ask the ladies and gentlemen present if such a law exists? You are the experts. Tell me: is there such a law?'

The judge indicated to the prosecutor to continue. But she broke in.

'I trusted you. But I went to the law school and asked them. The teachers there are better than you lot. One of the professors helped me call some of my daughter's classmates. There was a boy named Su. He liked my girl. His phone was switched off. We spent the night looking for him, but by the time we found him the next day the sun was coming up. Him. My daughter's murderer.' She was pointing at me. 'His aunt got home that morning and as soon as she saw the blood she called the police. But she was already dead.'

She looked stunned by the reality of what she'd just said, as if this was the first time she was hearing the terrible news. She began wailing. People looked around the court, not knowing what to do, until her relatives pulled her back to her seat. But she started screaming.

'This isn't over! I will never give up! I'll write to the mayor! There must be justice!'

The judge pummelled his gavel. The whole scene shocked me, it was playing out as if the fault lay with the police, not me. I was upset and even thought of standing up and shouting at them myself. The prosecutor desperately resumed his questioning so that the policeman could make a quick and gloomy exit. My lawyer had no intention of putting any questions to him.

My aunt was supposed to have been called in, but instead the prosecutor read out a transcript of a formal interview. Next came the two guards from the military academy. Their cheeks were puffy and red, but as soon as they saw me their eyes turned cold, like wolves. They were angry. How were they supposed to know? 'Isn't it your job to keep watch, not just stand around?' their boss would have roared back, thumping the table.

The first guard admitted to having seen a girl entering the compound, the second wasn't sure.

'You swap shifts at 3.00, correct?'

'Correct.'

'I believe this was a premeditated murder,' the prosecutor said, pointing at me.

'I never said it wasn't,' I said, standing up.

My lawyer silenced me and, with a feigned look of pain, sat back down.

The day's session finished with the identification of the switchblade and other pieces of evidence. As the officers led me away, Kong Jie's mother rushed over and scratched at my face. Her relatives followed behind and pinched me too. The officer grabbed my arm and dragged me off to stop me from charging back. I looked away as we left and saw Kong Jie's mother kicking out like a naughty child, before collapsing in tears.

'My girl, my girl!'

Everyone was trying to help her, but this worsened her tantrum.

It felt so ritualised. Maybe she felt she had to perform like this to prove she was a real mother. But I knew this wasn't real suffering. Real suffering would break through in the moments she spent alone while looking at photos of her daughter. Even then, the grief wouldn't produce tears, only a hollow feeling, as if her organs had been spooned out of her body.

The trial was over in a matter of days. My lawyer argued that the case should be treated as a matter of legal technicality, while the prosecutor contended this was premeditated murder in the first degree from which I had tried to abscond. It was straightforward logic. The judge agreed. He asked if I had anything to add; I said no.

A few days later I was led back into court. Everyone stood along with the judge as he relayed decision in his beautifully modulated voice. I was swimming in unfamiliar words; I could barely understand any of it. Just as I thought we were nearing a conclusion, he licked his finger and turned to a new page.

'Just read the last sentence,' I said.

He stopped and his glasses slid down his nose. The officer beside me kicked me in the shin.

Finally, the judge came to the verdict: the defendant was guilty of murder in the first degree.

Sentence: the death penalty.

Grievous bodily harm, fixed prison term of ten years.

Rape, eight years.

The judge had barely finished when I felt another sharp kick to the shin. I bent over in pain.

At least it was all finished. But then he started reading again. Now we came to the civil action brought by the victim's family. The court had taken into account my economic circumstances and decided I was unable to pay compensation, so none was to be granted.

A thud sounded behind me as someone fell to their seat. In this instance the court had judged her rather than me. I did regret killing her daughter in some ways, but if I hadn't committed a murder so intolerable to our hypocritical society, what would have been the point?

The Appeal

Two days later Ma came. She was still avoiding people and when they bumped into her she would say, 'My son's going to be dead soon too. I don't owe anyone anything.'

She looked at me and placed a selection of different drinks and a large bag of roasted chicken wings before me.

'Son, you were right. If you don't eat well, there's no point in making money.' But there was a screen between us. She gestured at a guard as if he was a waiter. 'These are for my son.'

'I'm afraid all gifts must be registered.'

'Then please register these for me.'

'You have to do it yourself.'

Displeased, she put them back in her bag. 'Son, if you want a bird's nest or bear paw, Mama can get them for you. My money is worthless without you.'

'Save it. You need it to start a new family.'

Yes, I was being cruel, but what else could I say? Ma's tears burst forth like a fountain. It was the first time I'd ever seen her cry like that.

She cocked her head and said, 'Mama is going to get you out.'

'Impossible.'

'I don't believe that.'

I didn't say anything. In one short month she'd become a stubborn ox. Maybe this was the first time in her life she really had something worth fighting for.

'Wait,' she said, grabbing her bag and striding out of the visitors' room. After fifty metres she stopped, turned and called back, 'You've lost so much weight.'

Ma came back two days later with a squat, bald lawyer.

'I don't understand, but you can explain it to my son.'

'Here's the thing, boy. We want to appeal on your behalf to the Supreme Court. But we need your consent.'

'I'm not appealing.'

'But it's your right. Why wouldn't you?'

'I know.'

'My name is Li, everyone knows me. Mr Li has got three men off death row.'

'I know, but there's no need.'

Ma beat at the glass, first with her hands and then with her head. I watched her eyes, nose and teeth contort as they came at me, before pulling back again.

'Just some cooperation,' she howled.

'OK,' I said, nodding.

But I started regretting it as soon as I got back to my

cell. I was like a character in a novel who has gone to drown themselves in the sea but who meets an old friend on the beach and is kidnapped by the conversation.

I couldn't tell my mother I wanted to die.

From then on, Ma and the lawyer came and left on a cloud of dust, too busy for niceties. I was the emperor and they were the loyal ministers. One day the lawyer arrived with an official document from the A— Province People's Hospital, dated five years previously, which described the after-effects of a wound I had sustained to the head. Symptoms included headaches, hysteria and signs of neurosis. I told them it never happened.

'We have the word of a doctor,' the lawyer said, pulling out a transcript, on which was written:

Q: *Did you write this medical record?*

A: Yes.

Q: *The proof?*

A: That's my signature.

'I've never been to the People's Hospital,' I said.

He rapped on the counter, exasperated. I understood.

'You listen to me from now on. Your answers are

limited to yes or no. That's it.'

I would say yes to everything. He was there to remind me of my story.

He looked satisfied, but before leaving he asked one more time, 'Can you tell me why you were admitted to hospital?'

I didn't know what to say. He looked disappointed.

'Someone hit you on the head with a brick as you were walking through the night market during your New Year holidays.'

'Right.'

'You must remember your injuries.'

We were dicing with death here. I was under no illusions that there'd be a miracle, but my lawyer went on to outline the five potential lines of 'escape'. He made it sound as if the death penalty was the least likely of outcomes.

1. Judicial appraisal.
2. Apportion some of the responsibility to society.
3. Change of date of birth.
4. That there was in fact no intent to commit rape.
5. A leniency plea based on having given myself up.

'But I didn't give myself up,' I said.

'Yes, you did,' he replied firmly. 'Upon your arrest

you voluntarily made contact with the police. Before your arrest you wrote three options on three separate hundred-*yuan* notes. One of those was to give yourself up. Which means the intent was there. You also called your assistant class monitor Li Yong to tell him where you were. For a kid your age, the class monitor and assistant class monitors are the highest possible levels of authority. This shows your desire to repent to those in charge.'

'I was fed up with the game.'

'Which amounts to turning yourself in.'

My mother came back a few days later with a spring in her step. She was waving wildly with excitement. Anyone would think she had in her possession a paper granting my release.

'You must thank your mother,' the lawyer said. 'I've never seen such persistence.'

'What's happened?' I said.

'Kong Jie's mother has agreed to file a petition for clemency,' he said.

'How come?' I said.

'Your mother offered her seven hundred thousand,' he said.

'Where did she get that from?' he said.

'I have savings. I sold the shop and the house. It was

enough,' Ma said.

'Your mother also borrowed twenty thousand,' he said.

'You've already given it?' I said.

'Not all of it. The first instalment is sitting safely with Kong Jie's uncle. She still hasn't promised personally,' he said.

'How could she? I killed her daughter. Why would she grant me mercy?' I said.

'She didn't agree at first,' Ma said. 'But I said to her, "I'm a single mother, so are you. We both only have one child. Will my son's death bring your daughter back? I'd have swapped him for your daughter if I could, but that's not how it works. Can't you let him live, seeing as we are both alone in this world?"'

'I said to her, "It's not easy raising a daughter'," the lawyer said. '"She was on the cusp of becoming a woman. It's our fault, no doubt about it. But it's done now. We have to look on the positives. This is a chance to display a moral magnanimity rarely seen these days. Beg for mercy on his behalf and you will have saved two lives. This woman's and her son's. They will do their utmost to repay you – compensate you, I mean. They will for ever be indebted to your grace."'

'And she agreed?'

'No, she got someone to beat your mother up at first,'

he said. 'Your mother kowtowed and begged them to name a price. Mrs Kong ignored her, until one of her relatives could stand it no longer and offered to help your mother to her feet. But your mother refused and Mrs Kong spat on her.'

Ma looked down. The lawyer continued.

'Your mother suggested money. Three hundred thousand wasn't enough, so she said five hundred. When they refused that, it became seven hundred. Ten thousand, twenty thousand at a time. But no reaction. Your mother fainted. Mrs Kong said, "How do you expect me to react now?"'

'We're not sure if it's a definite yes,' Ma said.

'It was a definite yes,' the lawyer said. 'All we need is for you to repent in court.'

The Verdict

Five months later the Supreme Court of Appeal held the second trial back in the same courtroom. The fact that there wouldn't be a third trial gave me some comfort. I was fed up with being chased through the labyrinth. I was me, not some fictional character. Time once again felt inexhaustible, a cataract growing across my eyes. I'd started gnawing at my wrist, which the prosecutor argued was an attempt to escape proper punishment through suicide.

I recognised him, the prosecutor, but he, of course, didn't know me. His shoulders were narrow and he was stretched tall like a shoulder pole. He sat in the court with one leg over the other, flicking through his papers every now and again, reminding himself of the most salient points. As soon as the trial began, I knew at once he wasn't taking it particularly seriously. But he nevertheless possessed a foolish self-confidence. He thought he could make a last-minute lunge to clutch at the Buddha's feet. But still he let slip three gaping yawns. He must have spent the night drinking and playing dice, perhaps with his arms around a woman. His ears were filled with the sounds of karaoke.

After my lawyer had laid out our case, he asked the court to produce the medical examiner's report. Dr Tears was brought out again and through my lawyer's questioning was forced to admit that no traces of semen were found in the girl's vagina.

'That doesn't mean he didn't intend to rape her,' the medical examiner contended.

Clearly this was an unsatisfactory assumption.

'Considering the circumstances,' my lawyer replied, 'had my client wished to rape the victim, he would have. And traces of such an act would have remained. Was the victim's hymen intact?'

'Yes,' the medical examiner replied.

'But during the first trial the defendant admitted to attempted rape. And the conclusion of the court was the attempt had been aborted,' the prosecutor said.

'The court must place most weight on evidence, rather than confessions. Imagine that a young man of sixty-two kilos wishes to rape a defenceless girl weighing only thirty-nine kilos. Why should the attempt have been aborted?'

'The law does not allow for conjecture. That is a question for the defendant.' The prosecutor was suddenly aware of his mistake.

I stood up. 'I never wanted to rape her, and neither did I try.'

The courtroom erupted; I had withdrawn a confession. My lawyer sat down in silence. He must have been feeling pleased with himself.

'Then why did you confess to rape during police questioning?' the presiding judge cut in.

I didn't answer.

The prosecutor stood up. 'I would like to ask the defendant what evidence he has to prove he did not intend to rape the victim.'

He was obviously feeling flustered to ask such a dumb question.

'Objection,' my lawyer interrupted.

But I raised my handcuffed hand. 'I masturbated not long before Kong Jie came to my place. Sexual relations with her therefore didn't cross my mind.'

'And do you have proof?' the prosecutor declared.

'No. Apart from what it says in the medical examiner's report.'

'It doesn't prove you weren't thinking about it.'

'I'm sorry, I wasn't thinking about it. Had I been, there was nothing to stop me going through with it.'

'You didn't think of it?' The prosecutor was losing his sense of propriety.

'I thought about it, but I never intended to actually do it.'

'Why not?'

'For the sake of purity.'

'Purity?'

'I killed her for the sake of killing her. I didn't want to sully that with anything impure.'

My lawyer finally cut in. 'This proves that despite the depraved nature of his crime, he did not act completely without principle.'

He then read out a statement that had been signed by over four hundred neighbours, classmates and acquaintances. They swore upon their good names that I cherished the old and weak – that I was fundamentally honest. They collectively appealed to the court to show leniency.

My lawyer began to read each name in turn, but the judge broke him off. He was trembling, as if to say that these few lowly sheets of paper were unworthy of the mighty will of the people displayed thereon. Ma and the lawyer must have used a lot of sweets and red envelopes of money to obtain those signatures. My lawyer probably started it off with a couple of dozen signatures of his own before soliciting friends and relatives.

Then came a statement from my aunt. She had reflected on her own behaviour, her inflated sense of superiority, her rough and arbitrary manner. She had failed to recognise that I was still only a young boy, she said, and in doing so had subconsciously contributed to my destruction. Her statement went on to outline twenty or so instances of discriminatory and unjust treatment, including purposefully leaving fifty cents out on the table to see if I would steal it, only giving me leftovers to eat, etc.

After my lawyer finished reading, he came over to me, his brow wrinkled, his eyes shining fiercely like torches, as if he didn't know me.

'I want you to answer my following questions honestly.'

'OK.'

'Do you swear?'

'I swear.'

'Was it not the case that you really wanted to kill your aunt?'

'You could say that.'

'Yes or no?'

'Yes,' I said, raising my voice.

'Objection. These are leading questions,' the prosecutor began.

The judge told my lawyer to be careful. But he was already in the throes of an intensely passionate performance. He thrust his hands his pockets and began pacing.

Suddenly: 'Why did you kill her?'

'Bigotry.'

'What do you mean, bigotry?'

'I was an outsider. They looked down on me. It was an all-encompassing, overwhelming bigotry.'

'And how did it make you feel?'

'That I was already a criminal. Every day, they stripped me naked.'

'Did it make you want to cry?'

I looked up at him in bafflement. He kept signalling with his eyes for me to speak.

'Could you explain this feeling of pain to us more clearly?' he continued.

I didn't know how to answer, so I lowered my gaze and said nothing. Maybe I shook my head.

'Look,' he said, pointing at me like a piece of evidence, 'he struggles to put the humiliation into words.

'So why didn't you kill your aunt?' he continued just as suddenly.

She wasn't worth it, I thought.

'Because you couldn't kill someone as strong as her,' my lawyer began answering for me. 'So you chose to kill a classmate, to frighten your aunt. To tell her you weren't such a pushover. It was your childish way of getting back at her.'

The prosecutor thumped the table and decried this as mere sophistry. The judge replied with his gavel. But my lawyer was in mid-performance. The hands went back in the pockets and he strode over to the public gallery. He looked at each of them in turn, with purpose. When they were all suitably stunned, he lifted his pen and began pointing at them individually.

'You are all guilty.' He paused before continuing. 'You give him pressure to do well in his exams. You look down on him because of where he's from. You roll your eyes, you ignore him, you treat him like an outsider, call him a peasant. To you, he is a slave. You make him part of an underclass. You don't give two hoots about him. In fact, you think he is an imposition on your safe little world. You think he deserves this life. And you feel no guilt about it, am I right? Now you can't forgive him. But let me ask you something. What gave you the right to sit there all stately, like emperors? Does it make you feel good?'

Almost shaking with fright at his own words, he sat back down.

But the prosecutor would not be outdone. He stood up.

'I agree with you. So perhaps we should be sentencing the aunt to death instead? Or how about all of us? Execute all of us. And set him free. Does that sound right?'

'Yes,' my lawyer replied, his voice husky. 'I agree completely.'

'Well, I don't. Because I don't think the situation is as you describe it. Not in the slightest. If the defendant merely wanted to scare his aunt, he could have killed her cat or dog or something. There was no need to involve anyone else. If he felt he needed to kill a classmate to prove his point, he didn't need to stab her thirty-seven times. And why put her in the washing machine? Why do you think he did that?'

He paused to give everyone time to think this through. He then pointed his long, bony finger at me, like a gun. I cocked my head. The trembling finger took its aim at me again. I couldn't escape.

'Hatred!' he cried. 'Bitter hatred. He committed such a cruel act out of hate for Kong Jie. That is the only explanation.'

He asked me if I had asked her out. No, I said. He asked again if she had rejected me. I said no. He was happy with my answers, as if this somehow made me more of a criminal than if I had said yes. He then began his own speech, drawing on the theories of Freud, Jung, inferiority complexes, princesses and plain, ugly desire. He had memorised sayings and quotations, while trying to convey the gushing fluidity of a waterfall. When he hit a verbal blockage, he glanced down at his notes. But each blockage brought about a new cascade of bluster. He finished by collapsing back into his chair, as if coming down with some grave malady.

Upon the prosecutor's insistence, my aunt was finally brought into the court. She took a few steps and stopped. It was as if she was the one on trial. Eventually, she tottered up into the witness stand. She didn't look up. Her brow glistened with sweat.

The prosecutor asked her to repeat what she had seen at the scene of the crime and her voice quivered through the description. The courtroom frightened her, I could tell, but everyone mistook it for the horror of the memory.

'The defence counsel has argued that it was your unjust treatment of the defendant that caused him to commit the crime. What is your response?'

My aunt's huge frame convulsed (like a skyscraper about to fall). 'That is incorrect.'

With that one sentence she made her betrayal, abandoning all that Ma and the lawyer had persuaded her to say.

'So that wasn't the reason for his crime?'

'It has nothing to do with me.'

'Did you mistreat your nephew?'

'I wouldn't call it mistreatment.'

'Then what would you call it?'

'They should be more generous. His mother asked me to look after him, said he was my responsibility. I even moved out of my own home so as not to disrupt his studies. He put on at least five kilos while he was living with me. Ask him.'

My lawyer stood up to speak but I raised my hand. The judge motioned for me to speak.

'Aunt, where's your jade Buddha?'

'What jade Buddha?'

'The one taped to the bottom of your safe.'

'I don't own a jade Buddha.'

'Yes, you do. How many gifts have you and uncle received over the years?'

The woman looked dumbstruck and then flopped to the ground, as if in a bad soap opera. A few people rushed to help her up. No one felt more sorry for themselves in that moment than she did. But now she wouldn't dare talk about compensation. Ma paid her back a long ago. Whatever. She got what she deserved.

Next came our old neighbour Mr He. It must have been a while since he'd been let out into such a large space and he was clearly itching to say his piece. He spiced his descriptions liberally, filling them with invented misdemeanours on my part: 'You could say, he's done it all.' His lips furled, unleashing scorn as if he was the government. But to me he was just a putrid, decaying old man.

'You hit me,' I said.

'No, I didn't.'

'Yes, you did. You dug your nails into my neck, cursed me, slapped me across the face. You humiliated me to the core.'

'Nonsense.'

'You hit me whenever you felt like it.'

This was fun. He didn't know how to stop me. I could see him clench his fists.

'Is your dog dead?' I asked. This took him by surprise. 'I fed him rat poison.'

The old man's face went red and he began shouting.

'Are you fucking human? You had to kill the dog too?'

My lawyer sighed. I was being childish, probably. The prosecutor smiled. Surely nothing proved the ruthless cruelty of a killer like this?

After that a police officer was called. He said that normally even the toughest thugs lost it in prison, cried, asked to see their families. I was the only one to remain calm and detached, as if none of it bothered me.

'His only request was for a McDonald's.'

'It was a KFC,' I said.

Last Words

As soon as my lawyer suggested a plea for leniency, the public prosecutor scrambled to his feet and cried that such a crime could never be pardoned. As the scales tipped to the left, my lawyer decided to change tactics and add weight to the right, which he did by producing a certificate signed by a midwife stating that I had not yet turned eighteen. The prosecutor argued for an investigation, including an inspection of our household registration documents and my school records, as well as witness testimonies and a trace of my mother's movements eighteen years ago. They weren't impossible requests. He simultaneously reminded my lawyer that pressuring a witness into giving false testimony was an offence under the law.

My lawyer then repeated his three-pronged argument about how I had willingly given myself up. This the prosecutor could not accept, because I had yet to express even a hint of remorse. The lawyer narrowed his eyes at me as if to say, I'm not doing this alone, kid. But the last thing I wanted to do was make such a performance in court.

'You feel no remorse, isn't that correct?' the prosecutor said.

The question was there to help me, but I just cocked my head. I didn't say yes, I didn't say no. I wanted to say yes.

'Why did you go looking for the police officer?' my lawyer asked.

My head was still cocked. The judge reminded me I was required to answer. I thought for a long time and then decided I'd better tell the truth.

'Because I came to the conclusion that they were so lousy they wouldn't catch me otherwise.'

My lawyer looked betrayed and flustered. He walked past me in the dock, thumped on the table and filed an application for a psychological examination.

He then produced a medical report stamped by the A— Province People's Hospital supposedly written five years previously. He began reading out loud the diagnosis: hysteria and neurosis mainly, peppered with quotations from seminal works of psychology for reinforcement. He expounded on the necessary nature of such expert testimony, arguing that the court's own examinations were inadequate, and that this medical certificate was in full accordance with the principles of objectivity as required by the judicial system. He then took out another paper, in which two professors of law had written in support of this appraisal. And he quoted: 'Our justice system should treat cases such as these as iron-clad. It is too late to conduct a medical appraisal after the death sentence has been carried out.'

The prosecutor laughed coldly. He dragged a comb through his already neat hair, guiding it with his other hand for protection. This was a standard tactic used by the defence. He then pointed at me and spoke to the rest of the room.

'Does he show any signs of mental illness?' He then turned to me. 'Are you sick?'

'Of course not.' I could sense the shock in the room.

'How do you know?' my lawyer growled, standing up.

'Shouldn't I know best?'

'That's what every mentally ill person says. That's the best proof, right there.'

His veins were popping as he thumped at the table. Laughter erupted in the public gallery.

'So do you need an appraisal or not?' the judge asked.

'No,' I said.

My lawyer threw his briefcase onto the table and looked as if he was about to storm out. Only a sense of his own self-importance stopped him and he asked for Kong Jie's mother to be brought in. He then looked across at me like a man who was about to die making his last desperate plea to be saved. I, however, had long wanted an end to this game. The person in the courtroom on trial wasn't me, but a machine designed to validate my lies.

Mrs Kong was wearing the same black ankle-length dress, but this time she had added a long blue scarf. Kong Jie's scarf. Holding back her tears, she read out a document apparently entitled *An Act of Mercy from One Mother to Another.* Everyone in the court wore grave expressions, listening without moving. Her performance that day was pretty good; her tone, the balance between emotion and restraint, it was all exquisite. My lawyer must have written the script for her, but somehow it must also have touched a nerve (it was so unlike her wild shouting of before). My lawyer was like a songwriter watching the performance from his position in the audience as he seemed to tap his finger in time. People wiped tears from their eyes.

But I had to stop her. 'This is a financial transaction.'

I watched as the paper floated from her hand like a white crane. Her thin, solemn frame began to tremble. She closed her eyes, opened them, and then fell backwards. People rushed to help. Saliva frothed around her mouth and her body twitched as if she was having an epileptic fit. The court was filled with noise like school breaking for the day: people fidgeted, talked, anxious and unsure of what to do. Then it hit them. Together:

Kill him!

Kill him! Kill him!

Kill him! Kill him! Kill him!

I looked up at the ceiling and then out at the courtroom. It was small, like a theatre box. People far in the distance were waving their fists and all that was left were the yellow seats and dark green banisters. On the wall to the side was fastened a Western-style lamp which was on but gave out only the weakest light. No one thought to switch it off. There will come a day, when everyone has gone, when all that is left is the dancing dust.

'Kill me,' I said, returning to reality.

My eyes showed I was sincere. My lawyer had stuffed his papers into his briefcase and taken his place as a spectator. The public prosecutor was stunned; his body shook. Eventually he began reading from a report, his voice almost singing. What I heard was 'vicious in the extreme', 'utterly devoid of conscience', 'total disregard for the law and human life', 'ruthless methods', 'serious consequences', 'grave danger to society', 'public indignation if we don't hand down the death sentence'.

The courtroom exploded in applause as he finished and continued for some time before stopping abruptly. They felt the amorphous loneliness just as I did.

The judge asked for my response.

'I want to tell the public prosecutor that I actually passed him in the street the day I bought the switchblade. And I thought about killing him. But my plans were already fixed.'

Confused, he looked down.

Just then a lion-like roar broke through the silence. 'Why did you kill my daughter and not someone else!'

'I had to kill someone.'

'You could have killed a corrupt official or a thug. Why did you have to kill my daughter?'

'Because she was worth it.'

'What do you mean by that?' the judge said.

'Because she was beautiful, kind, clever. She had a future, but she had a difficult childhood, lost her father young. She's your sweetheart, all of you.'

'You animal!' the public prosecutor cried.

'So you did it out of hate?' the judge continued.

'No, I did it for a reaction. I've read the newspapers, magazines. I know how much attention a vicious murder case gets. Especially if the victim is a child, student or young woman. Even ugly girls become precious beauties, kind and loved, if they are murdered. If plain girls get that treatment, reactions to the death of a girl like Kong Jie, who was pretty much perfect, would be more exaggerated. Then I worried the story wouldn't be big enough, so I stabbed her thirty-seven times. I planned it all carefully. She trusted others easily, was a good girl. You guys, you all live with these supposed lofty ideals. A pretty vase like her gets smashed? I knew you'd be rushing to express unparalleled anger and emotion. You would agonise over the fact that you couldn't do to me what I did to her. That you couldn't dismember me.'

'You killed her to become famous?' the public prosecutor asked.

'No, I just wanted to make sure I handed you enough motivation to come and catch me. I killed someone you couldn't tolerate to be killed so that you would put all your energy and resources into hunting me down. Get everyone involved. But you couldn't do it. You got lazy. So I gave myself up to the police.'

'You murdered her so that you could go on the run?' the judge asked.

'Yes. Running away is the only way to feel alive. You're the cats, I'm the mouse. Mice are clever, strong; they are streamlined, carry no extra weight. They are almost mathematical in their beauty. I've been longing to feel such nervous energy, such pressure.'

'Don't you have your college entrance exams soon?' the judge said. 'Couldn't you throw yourself into the anxiety of studying?'

'I was secretly assigned to the military academy a long time ago. My uncle is head of the dean's office.'

'You could have chosen to put your energies into something positive.' The judge again.

'I tried. I put everything into being an exceptional

student. But those things are like water cast out in the desert, they evaporate quickly. Whenever I started something, I would picture its inevitable ending. An apple becomes pips in the trash. While everyone is making toasts during their feast, a cat paces in the kitchen waiting for the scraps. Take love. Fireworks exploding in the air. We're like impotent men trying to have sex, we're cheating ourselves. We want to believe the sky is lit up by the sparks of romantic connection when actually it's just black. Our lives are simply a long turn to old age and decrepitude until we can't even wipe our own arses. It's undignified. Then once we're dead along comes a dog one day, digs up our bones and plays with them. We're nothing more than decaying corpses.'

'What do you think the point of life is?' the prosecutor asked.

'Exactly. There is no point. If I'd killed you instead, yours would have had some meaning at least.'

He banged his hand against the table. I really thought I'd set him off, but I continued.

'I'm not here today to play God and tell you what life is really about. All I'm trying to say is I may be young but my soul is exhausted. This is my reality. I lost faith in it all a long time ago. I know swans have nothing to do with poetry. Why are they always flying? Because they're like pigs, avoiding the cold, looking for food.

We're no different. We're not better than animals, we display all the same disgusting behaviours. We're just aware of it, that's all. We hunt for food, plunder territories, calculate resources. We're completely controlled by our primal sexual urges. We do it all, but feel ashamed. We invented meaning just like we invented underpants. But once we see through these fake meanings, it all slips away until the word no longer makes sense.

'This false enlightenment made me detached, passive, bleak even. My life started to fall apart. I took to lying for hours as if paralysed. No miracles filled my days. Each was as unchanging as the one that went before. Time stood still, or moved achingly slowly, like pouring concrete. Every day was death by drowning. I couldn't breathe. I couldn't move. I felt absolute terror for no apparent reason. I took to crying. One day, when I could stand it no longer, I made a decision: seeing as I had no power over my life, I'd give it to you. I couldn't choose myself, but I'd give the choice to you. You chase, I run. It was that simple. Imagine an animal at the bottom of the food chain: everything is a constant competition, a hunt for food. The thought replenished me. Life is pointless after all; it's all the same, no matter what you do. It's all destructive ultimately. But at least this would prevent me from having to face the passing of time alone. I wanted to put up a protective barrier between myself and time. I used to think, wouldn't it be cool to go to war, or become an outlaw – that way I could satisfy my private desire to kill in the name of something greater. I thought of rescuing a damsel, like a knight in some martial arts novel, but then I realised no one would come miles looking for me to help them find retribution. No, killing your perfect sweetheart was my best option. I went on the run, dropping clues, like an animal leaves a trail of scent, so that you might find me. I was happy; my time was filled. I could feel it in my body. I was living a fruitful life. My performance was perfect. But you let me down.'

I was finished. I lifted my handcuffs and with great difficulty scratched the itch on the back of my neck. Everyone watched, dumbstruck. I was perverse, frightening, and yet somehow my conclusions made sense. I was feeling pretty good about my speech and even half expected someone to come over and pour me some water. After a while, a noise, a realisation, broke through the silence.

'No!'

It was the prosecutor. He pulled at his tie, jumped up and pointed at me.

'You are pure evil! Suddenly I can understand why people kill for money or desire. Compared to you, they are worthy of our respect! They still operate according to society's norms and our normal ways of thinking. But you! You are an attack on our very way of life, our traditions and the beliefs we rely on to live.'

I nodded. He stared at me as if I was a monster. Then came his screams, like those of a terrified child.

'The judge has the final say. I beg you, Your Honour, give this young man the death penalty. At once. Have him executed at once! I can feel his insidious thinking spreading and multiplying. He will only serve as inspiration to other helpless young people. He is a danger to our society. He will terrorise the whole world. I beg you! For all of us, for humankind, kill him at once!'

No response. Everyone sat in their seats.

I raised my handcuffed hands, looked up and spoke calmly.

'Yes. Shoot me.'

They led me to a new cell. The judgement came quickly and was no surprise. Documents pertaining to my case must have been rushed between government departments, from the District Court to the High Court, the High Court to the Supreme Court, which then prodded the High Court, which in turn prodded the District Court. The guards were handed a letter and they reported to their section manager, who then reported to the section chief, who then reported to the vice-procurator of the court, who then reported to his superior, the presiding judge. The death sentence would no doubt take months to process, maybe even a year. Probably it would be done by shooting, maybe by lethal injection. Whatever. I was waiting for my last supper. As for explaining the case to the outside world, they'd no doubt come up with their own explanation. Attempted robbery? Exam pressure? Social exclusion? Something suitable to propagate to the masses. They sure as hell wouldn't let people know it was out of boredom. A desire to play cat and mouse. That that was my reason for killing her.

My original plan consisted of four parts:

Purpose: Relief.
Method: Escape.
Technique: Murder.
Funds: Ten grand.

This is the full record of my last words. Let it be recorded in history that once lived such a person.

Goodbye.

Acknowledgements

I would like to thank Marysia Juszczakiewicz and Tina Chou at Peony Literary Agency, Oneworld Publications, my translator, Anna Holmwood, and Julia Lovell, who made the English-language edition of the book possible.

This book has been selected to receive financial assistance from English PEN's Writers in Translation programme, supported by Bloomberg and Arts Council England. English PEN exists to promote literature and its understanding, uphold writers' freedoms around the world, campaign against the persecution and imprisonment of writers for stating their views, and promote the friendly cooperation of writers and free exchange of ideas.

Each year, a dedicated committee of professionals selects books that are translated into English from a wide variety of foreign languages. We award grants to UK publishers to help translate, promote, market and champion these titles. Our aim is to celebrate books of outstanding literary quality which have a clear link to the PEN charter and promote free speech and intercultural understanding.

In 2011, Writers in Translation's outstanding work and contribution to diversity in the UK literary scene were recognised by Arts Council England. English PEN was awarded a threefold increase in funding to develop its support for world writing in translation.

www.englishpen.org